Leicester Writes
Short Story Prize 2017

First published 2017 by Dahlia Publishing Ltd
6 Samphire Close Hamilton
Leicester LE5 1RW
ISBN 9780995634428

Selection copyright © Dahlia Publishing 2017

Copyright of each piece lies with individual authors © 2017

The moral right of the authors has been asserted.

All rights reserved. No part of this publication may be reproduced, stored in
or introduced into a retrieval system, or transmitted, in any form, or by any
means (electronic, mechanical, photocopying, recording or otherwise)
without the prior written permission of the publisher. Any person who does
any unauthorized act in relation to this publication may be liable to criminal
prosecution and civil claims for damages.

Printed and bound by Grosvenor Group

This book is sold subject to the condition that it shall not, by way of trade or
otherwise, be lent, re-sold, hired out, or otherwise circulated without the
publisher's prior consent in any form of binding or cover other than that in
which it is published and without a similar condition including this
condition being imposed on the subsequent purchaser.

A CIP catalogue record for this book is
available from The British Library

CONTENTS

Foreword
REBECCA BURNS

John Steinbeck once wrote:

"If there is a magic in story writing, and I am convinced there is, no one has ever been able to reduce it to a recipe that can be passed from one person to another. The formula seems to lie solely in the aching urge of the writer to convey something he feels important to the reader. If the writer has that urge, he may sometimes, but by no means always, find the way to do it."

As Chair of Judges for the inaugural Leicester Writes Short Story Competition, I was lucky enough to read stories that managed to capture that aching, magical urge of the writer. Stories that conveyed magic and presented it, like a gift, to the reader. I've travelled alongside a family as they journeyed to the seaside, a terrible secret lurking in the background (*We Went There*); have held my breath as a woman is interrogated about the whereabouts of her absent, vulnerable mother (*Switching off the Metronome*); and been fully immersed in the peevish, rich world of malevolent spirits (*Aunty*). The stories mentioned took the top three spots in the Leicester Writes competition and demonstrate fully Steinbeck's comment that a writer might "find the way" to create a little bit of magic.

But how do these writers do it? In other words, what makes a short story work? How can a piece of writing really *pop* and grab the reader by the throat or the heart or the stomach and make time stand still? We've all read stories where we're transported and enthralled, and we've all read stories where a writer hasn't quite managed it, where we're left feeling slightly unsatisfied. But could we say exactly why we feel like that?

The most powerful stories I've read contain different, intoxicating elements but are all brilliantly done. I've read stories where there is a killer first line, a real humdinger – it snares you and your eyes are pulled down the rest of the page, like a fish on an inverted rod. You're dragged to the bottom and then you bounce back up again, onto the next page. The winning story, *Aunty*, by C. G. Menon has such a first line: "It wasn't till after we burnt her that Leila began to cause trouble." I was immediately intrigued and, I'm delighted to say, the rest of the story is just as wonderful.

Other stories work because they drop the reader straight into a fully-formed, fleshed out world. For the next two thousand words or so, the reader inhabits a moment in the life of a character but knows, convincingly, that there is a world beyond that on the page. Stories like this offer a glimpse or a snapshot of a life and the reader feels almost regretful when the story comes to an end. They want to know more. I always feel like that after reading Sarah Hall or Anthony Doerr, or the late, great, Carol Shields. You must have your favourites, too.

There's not much space in a short story so writing them can be very technical. Writers obviously have to make every word count, and there's no room for baggage. Backstories don't have the space to develop, so characters have to be drawn sharply. Settings must resonate in only a few lines. When it's done well, a strong short story will shine, be luminous.

I hope you will find something that shines for you in this collection. We judges enjoyed reading through the longlist and picking the shortlist, and there was a healthy and good-natured debate about which stories should win and be placed. I hope you will agree with our selection. Each writer in this collection was able, as Steinbeck said, to act on an aching urge to convey something important to the reader.

Aunty
C. G. MENON

It wasn't till after we burnt her that Leila began to cause trouble. It started early, while Gupta's crematorium smell was still tweaking our lungs and Leila was sifting in the ice-cream tub on Mohini's windowsill.

While she was alive, Leila had soothed our nightmares. She'd kissed our foreheads and left the bathroom light on to keep away the pontianaks; she'd bandaged our knees and helped with our sums. But now that she was dead, all that changed. She knotted the brothers' ties into tangles instead; she tossed the sisters' jewellery into the talcum powder box and wound the clocks backwards each night. Our dreams stretched thin as rice paper as we overslept and the cook swore among his saucepans while our breakfast went cold.

'Wah! She's in a plastic tub only? You need glass, Mohini-child. That will fix her.'

Aunty Bibi's long, quivering nose had smelt trouble all the way from next door. She arrived three days after the funeral, muttering Cantonese curses and stumping her way over the calla lilies. She dropped a box of laddoo on the kitchen table, shooed the pontianaks away from the door with such vigour that they soured the milk, then plumped into a dining chair to eat our cold nasi lemak. Bibi had cremated two husbands and stoppered them up in vases on

1

her polished windowsills. She knew how to keep ghosts in line.

'We're getting an urn soon, Bibi-Aunty. This was all we had.'

Mohini hadn't stopped crying since the funeral. She slept, she bathed, she scolded the younger children and licked kaya off her butter-knife all behind a glassy slide of tears. Ali-Driver and Ali-Hawker both came by to comfort her, one after another, and she pressed damp, luminous kisses into the creases of their necks. When she'd stripped the chauffeur's cap from one and the satay-sticks from the other, she led each boy into her bedroom and loosed those civet-cat screams she'd learnt from Meg Ryan at the Shaw Palace. We hoped one of these scuffles would clear the air, but after a few hours the liquid murmur returned and Mohini brought out a boy sodden and salty as a mermaid with all the coconut-oil sobbed out of his hair.

Bibi made her disapproval clear. She disliked the crumpled neckties, the dirty butter-knives and the way the younger children's dressing gowns scampered empty through the halls when our backs were turned.

'Well.' She swallowed the last chilli from the nasi lemak and coughed – a glorious, palate-scouring snort that made all the plates upend themselves and quiver in disgust. Bibi muttered something in Cantonese.

'Too delicate for snot, eh, Leila?'

Leila had been fastidious, even before she was a ghost. At the height of the flu her plump fingers had darted under her nose to catch any drips before they swung free. She'd never yawned or belched, and when she'd had hiccups she'd retreated to her room for two days and lived on stale fruitcake until they subsided.

'She'll make trouble, that one. You lock her up, Mohini-child.'

And with that Bibi kissed us all and sailed away through the lilies, leaving shipwreck behind her. That night there were footsteps in the attic and splashing in the bone-dry sinks. Leila's invisible fingers tugged our pillows away, tied birdseed to the kitchen-cats' tails and squeezed six lemons into her almirah to kill the silverfish that were eating her scarves.

And then it was a moist, fog-sopped morning and Mohini was screaming from her tiny bedroom. She slept in a dim little place, smelling of the Alis' loincloths mingled with her cotton underwear in a soup of warmth and curling hair.

'Mohini! Child, open the shutters.'

Bibi danced in a panic under the window, banging on the crumbling bricks. That nose of hers had been on the alert all night, much to the terror of the pontianaks scrambling in and out of her storm-drains to soak their two-clawed feet. She'd smelt the dust from Leila's footsteps and the cats' hissing rage, but it was the lemons that had her up at dawn. Their smell had reached right into her house and under her mosquito net, it had dragged her from her dreams and brought her through the dripping grass to hear Mohini's first scream.

'Mohini! Open up!'

One of the shutters crawled open to show a slice of bare throat and shoulders.

'My clothes are gone, Bibi-Aunty. Leila's cut them.'

And she had. One of the sisters reported that Mohini's miniskirts hung like spinach leaves from the hallway fan. A brother found the remains of her t-shirts soaking amongst the swamp weed and Mohini topped it all off by mournfully handing her underwear out through the window, to show us how every opening had been sewn shut with Leila's tiny, perfect stitches.

'Mohini, child, you can't stay like that.' Bibi was practical, and worried about chills. 'Wear Leila's clothes, from the almirah. Just for today.'

Mohini looked doubtful. Leila had spent hours tailoring those clothes into the shape she'd yearned for, nipping in where she didn't nip and tucking out where she'd never tucked. She'd hemmed jackets and pinned trousers, had peeled her tights off and darned them every evening in the hope they'd somehow transform her thighs. Each of us, creeping into Leila's almirah for games of hide-and-seek, had breathed in camphor and the sadness of clothes that had never quite fit. Now, the sisters helped Mohini pull the doors open and an old Huntley & Palmers tin rattled off the shelf to spill a mouthful of pins onto her toes.

'Leila-Aunty, it's your own fault,' Mohini argued plaintively and began to browse through the clanking wire hangers.

When she came out in Leila's second-best yellow dress, in the tight-seamed stockings and white sash, she walked more slowly than before. It suited her, we agreed together, the way Leila's dress packed her into shape. Her miniskirts had left her inclined to flightiness, and had set the sisters a bad example.

'There, child.' Bibi was still standing on the flowerbed, arms and legs akimbo in case Leila was planning any more mischief. She clambered out and whisked some lint from Mohini's shoulder. 'You're decent again.'

But Mohini was more than just decent. Leila's skirt wrapped itself around her legs all day and shrank her steps. The sash pinched however we tied it, and when Ali-Driver came by she had to send him away because neither of them could understand how to loosen Leila's petticoat hooks.

And to make matters worse, Aunty Bibi had been right about the urn. The plastic ice-cream tub we'd carried in four days ago had begun to leak tiny flakes of ash. Leila drifted through the air, getting into the spices and under our tongues until Mohini's hair turned a premature, sprinkled grey and everything tasted of cinders. We closed the shutters to stop Leila from getting out and giving the swamp-ghosts ideas, and stifled in the muddy gloom.

'Mohini-Aunty, look at our sums, please.' The younger children clung to Mohini's legs, wadding themselves against yellow silk thighs they thought they remembered.

She didn't understand sums, she argued, slapping them away with an older-sister glare. But in the midday twilight the younger children became panicky, filled with a frail kind of love that left them clawing at her knees and tugging her hair out of its ponytail.

'Mohini-Aunty, the sums!'

One of them pulled at the pocket of her yellow skirt, ripping it and setting a tiny waterfall of Leila's belongings tumbling free. A worn-down pencil, a jumble of hair-grips and three cancelled train tickets.

'What's that?' Mohini plucked the tickets back, held them up to her eyes. The blurred light was giving her a squint and the same furrowed brow Leila had when the lamp wicks needed trimming.

'They're all to the airport,' she said, and frowned. 'When did she go there?'

We looked at each other, the brothers and the sisters swapping glances that slunk like fireflies in the rain. In the corner a mosquito coil glowed bright red, and one of the brothers stubbed it out.

'She didn't go, Mohini-Aunty,' one of us said. 'She didn't catch the trains.'

'And I'm not an aunty!' The spinning fan had tangled Mohini's hair into flossy hanks, and the older sisters quietly pinned them back with Leila's hair-grips. 'What happened to her?'

It was a brother, or perhaps a sister, who answered first.

'The mosquitoes, Aunty. When you were away at school, remember? The malaria.'

#

'I have a ticket!'

Leila planted her hands on her hips, spongy and stocking-less under her dress. She'd joined the crowd outside the shabby train station at dawn in her slippers and third-best apron, carrying whatever she'd grabbed from the house as we slept. A mop, a packet of flour and the younger children's arithmetic homework juggled for space in her wicker basket.

'Madam, it's quarantine. If you carry out the malaria, then what?' The guard was young and fresh as scrubbed bamboo cane, with his rifle stick-straight against the blackened, buzzing sky.

'Pah!' Leila snapped, dismissing malaria and quarantine alike with a snap of her fingers. She pushed him aside with her mop, leaving a splodge of wet soap to take the curl from his hair and the starch from his jacket. A stiff yellow banner had been pasted over the ticket office in the middle of the night and the tracks lounged shimmering and deserted except for a few bony dogs. Like Leila, everyone had booked their tickets weeks before and a crowd flocked along the road with little queasy cries like gulls in a storm. Businessmen carried bags and suitcases, flower-sellers balanced feathery sheaves of hibiscus petals on their heads and ayahs bundled children under their arms like chickens trussed for market. The sunlight was filmy, filtering through an immense cloud of mosquitoes that boiled above the patient hills.

Three miles away, that cloud of mosquitoes was rising in a bubbling funnel from a fish pond in our garden. The brothers, being the best at nature study, had been in charge this time. They'd spent weeks coaxing mosquitoes to the pond, ever since we'd found Leila's ticket in her shapeless handbag. They'd stretched their bare legs out by the water every evening to tempt mosquitoes grown hungry or sly, and every morning they'd rescued larvae from puddles that could dry up in the noontime sun. The sisters helped, too, covering the pool in a mat of swamp weed and snatching out any koi that put up its golden, gappy lips through the twisting stems.

Now, we sat cross-legged on the grass amongst fish bones delicate as ivory combs. A sister leant over and dabbled her fingers, stirring more mosquitoes to join the cloud that would cover the town for a week. It would smother the sun and dim the street lamps until three children died of malaria and one of fright, until the flower-sellers dropped their bundles to blossom by the roadside, until Leila missed her train and returned home just in time to correct our sums.

#

'But … the other tickets?' Mohini's tears had dried by now, leaving her cheeks cracked and pitted. We rubbed at her temples, soothing her. 'What happened?'

She stayed quite still while we told her, while we pinned her hair and straightened her sash. The second time, we explained, Ali-Hawker had promised Leila she could borrow his tricycle to get to the station. But a sister made sure the garden gate was swinging open as Ali brought the tricycle, tempting him into a shortcut through the hedges and into a draught of scented air spilling from Mohini's open window. That scent made him drop the handlebars and leave the wheels spinning amongst anthills and buddleias while he climbed in with a shaking need. Half an hour later his tricycle collapsed under Leila on the road, its hinges flying apart with the shock of Ali's first kiss and his discovery of what lay under the flightiness of Mohini's miniskirts.

The final time, Leila locked herself in the attic by mistake after a brother oiled the latch that had, in any case, been sticking for too long. She spent a night there with the civet-cats, peering out between strands of the attap roof while she caught the chill that would eventually kill her. The attic, we said, was strung with spiders in their silky webs and littered with the kiss-curls of dried-up centipedes. It was a place where things ended up; everything from toys to burnt saucepans, from the brothers' first wet dreams to the sisters' peaceable nightmares, from aunties to civet-cats.

#

By now, some things are different. We've shared the rest of Leila's clothes out, the ones that wouldn't fit Mohini, however she stitched. The jackets have been turned into dressing gowns, to replace the ones that still scamper shamefacedly in cupboards where they think nobody will notice. The scarves have gone to the brothers, in place of the neckties still knotted in tricky tangles about the door handles. We gave Aunty Bibi a skirt in return for one of her stoppered vases, and Leila now lives bottled up in glass on a stand of polished jambu wood.

And we wait.

We're decked out in scarves that smell of camphor and shirts that don't quite fit. We oversleep each morning; we turn our backs on the darkened corridors and tug our pillows straight and send the cook home to make nasi lemak for his own children. Ali-Hawker and Ali-Driver don't visit anymore and Mohini's nose has grown as long and troublesome as Leila's. Every night she darns her stockings in Leila's room, padding about barefoot over rusty pins and squeezed-out lemon peel. And we sit down in the oil-lamp blackness of the attic to play mah-jongg with the pontianaks, and we listen to those pulpy footsteps and we wait until our aunty decides to leave.

Switching Off the Metronome
SIOBHAN LOGAN

Mozart's Sonata in C is shrill today. As her voice once was. It's not often someone presses the doorbell, so I stumble to attention.

The male PC's in his early thirties and there's a blonde with pinned-up hair behind him. Their uniforms look crisp and dangerous, gadgets strapped everywhere. I clutch at my dressing gown.

'Can we come in, Miss Jennings?' he says again.

'Ah – yes. Maura's fine.'

They tell me their names, which I immediately forget. The woman smiles briskly as she steps into the hall but she's already surveying the place. Hard-edged as her bowler hat. That racing-flag tie and neon-yellow jacket.

Such a hideous outfit for a woman, my mother would have said. *Ugly as jazz.*

'So – you've found her then?' I say. 'Is she at the station?'

"Fraid not. No sightings yet. Why don't we have a chat while my colleague checks her room?'

'Oh I don't really – I haven't, you know, tidied.'

The thought of the bathroom is mortifying. But the WPC is already up the stairs.

He ushers me into my mother's sitting room as if I'm the guest. I'm ashamed to notice how shabby its gentility has become. Stained velvet. I must have been his age when I moved back in. Seven years that nibbled and unpicked us both like a family of voracious mice.

I scrabble to pick up the used tissues. He offers to make tea while I clear blankets off the sofa, but he can't find the kettle.

'Oh it's locked away. Sorry. She gets into everything. She'll eat kitchen roll if I leave it out. Hence the padlocks.'

I grab my bunch of keys from the sideboard, jingle them like a good warder.

'Ah, no worries.'

He sits with his notebook out. 'Has she wandered off before?'

I nod, hear myself gabbling the story again. How I woke up about six in the morning to find the front door ajar. And I looked everywhere, driving around for hours.

'I can't believe I forgot about the deadlock.'

'Easily done,' he says. 'What's that wooden object? Very ornate.'

'The metronome? It keeps you in time when you play.' So of course I have to show him.

'Oh, it's wind-up. Like old clocks.'

'Yes, this'll pretty much last forever.' Unclasping the walnut frontage, I release the pendulum. It's set to four-four. That must have been her last lesson, when she already knew what was coming. 'My mother was a music teacher.'

He talks over the metallic tick. 'So music is a great comfort to her.'

'Not really, she prefers television now. Cartoons.'

I hear the blonde open a drawer upstairs. 'What's she looking for?'

'Some clue, an address, anything you might have missed.'

As the pendulum flicks relentlessly, I'm clicked back into my mother's shouted corrections at her protégés: *No, no, no – do that again*. The soundtrack of my childhood. A scrape of furniture makes me jump.

'Do you play yourself?' He gestures to the piano.

'I was never any good. She stopped my lessons.'

This close, his aftershave dizzies me. I have to switch off the metronome, my mother's staccato eyes, her pulsing arias. Then the blonde bursts in.

'Miss Jennings? Can you tell us anything about this?'

I barely recognise the polka dots of her slip under the dirty red.

'Where? … what – is that blood?'

The nice young PC has to steady me.

#

In the interview room, a clock punches out time like the metronome. Five hours. My PC passes me another mug. The coffee is quite decent. I take a sip and heat flushes my body. But I daren't blow on it. I focus on keeping my story straight.

The inspector opposite steeples her fingers. Mother would have approved of the manicured nails. Two no-nonsense silver pips on the black epaulettes. At a nod from her, the PC switches on the cassette recorder and announces 'Interview resumed 3pm'.

'So you've remembered?' she cuts in.

'Yes, it was a nosebleed, all over her sheets, the mattress too.'

'Right.'

'She must've grabbed the slip and stuffed it behind the dressing table.'

'Why would she do that?'

'*Why?*' My voice cracks. 'Because she's lost her mind, gone doolally.'

She used exactly those words when she told me, over a Fortnum & Mason's cream tea. The tinkle of china punctuated our doom.

I put my head in my hands.

Unimpressed, the inspector slaps down two pharmacy packets. 'Tell me about these.'

'Th-they're mine.'

'Yes, I can read.'

'Antidepressants. And that one's … sleeping tablets.'

I glance uncertainly at the PC. He doesn't smile.

'From what I gather, your mother hardly recognises you. Why not put her in a home, get some professional care?'

Because she's my mother, I think. But I decide to go for the truth.

'Mummy made me promise … when she got the diagnosis. She was terrified, completely – she was only fifty-five.'

'Does your mother have life insurance?' she asks.

'What's that got to do with anything?'

'Well, let's see. How much *is* your carer's allowance?'

'Sixty-two pounds.'

'A *week*? So at thirty-four you give up a good job, your own house, to live on a pittance indefinitely … When did you last have a boyfriend?'

I squirm away from the PC's gaze. His voice is gentler.

'No one doubts you love your mother but … everyone has a breaking point.'

I remember at dawn, the brief, bright thought it might all be over. How I hammered it down.

'There are five locks on that front door,' he adds. 'The Yale, your chain-guard, two barrel-bolts top and bottom and the deadlock.'

'Quite the Fort Knox,' the inspector says. 'Rather a lot for a confused woman to get past, don't you think?'

'You can't be saying – that I … hurt my mother?'

The inspector doesn't answer but her face tightens with scrutiny. The PC chips in again.

'People who are in shock … sometimes forget things.'

I stare at the white collar above his stab vest. Immaculate. How I long to be that clean.

'Is there anything you haven't told us, Maura?'

'But if I did – *that* … where did I put the body?'

'You tell us,' the inspector says. 'Is there a body to find?'

My mind stumbles around the cluttered house. Under the stairs? The ditch at the bottom of the garden? The thought of the ditch makes me feel sick.

'No,' I say. 'No, no, *no*.'

She gives him the look and he switches off the machine. The clock continues to slice its seconds, a hand throwing knives.

#

The bed is a wooden shelf with a blue plastic mattress. Matching pillow. When I sit, the crunchy noise echoes between white tiled walls. The blanket is folded neatly. And there's a little niche for the steel toilet. Of course it smells of sadness and disinfectant. But I can't help admiring the hygiene of it all. There's worse at home.

I need to get used to institutions now, I think. There will always be a light on somewhere and voices rolling in from different corners of the building. The blanket is thin but the room's stuffy anyway. I look up at the window. No bars. Instead there are dozens of small squares of glass and I find the pattern mesmerising. Until I nod off. I sleep surprisingly well, for a time.

When I wake, they've turned off the main light. In the greyness, I reassemble my various confessions, place them like wonky handwritten quavers on a stave. The last one as warbly as my childish top-note.

It's that good cop, bad cop thing, I guess. As soon as the inspector stepped out for a comfort break, I crumbled. The PC switched the recorder back on.

'I really must advise you', he said, 'you should have some counsel for this.'

I waved the offer away. It was a relief to tell him. How I'd been dosing her with sleeping tablets to stop the night wanderings. My own early morning outings, time off for good behaviour. Coffee from the all-night garage, maybe a bench by the roundabout to watch sun-up. Birdsong, the drip of rain, sounds unregulated. An unlocked hour.

Then I admitted I never liked my mother. That was a whisper and he asked me to repeat it for the tape. He nodded as if he could understand. As if I might be forgiven. It'll be typed up by morning.

#

My PC waits at the custody desk beaming.

'I can't believe she got all the way to Brighton.'

He takes me down corridors I vaguely recognise from yesterday. No sign of the manicured inspector.

'She's right as rain, had a good feed and that. But guess what she was using for money?'

I spy her through the fire door, that Cheltenham Ladies' deportment and a battered handbag.

'Pegs,' I say.

'I know, we had a right laugh.'

17

In a pink and echoey room, my mother smiles. When I kiss her, she dabs vaguely at the spot. We were never good at that.

'What happens now?'

'You take your mum home. The Great Escape is over.'

So sentence is passed. We totter through the police car park. She makes that smacking noise with her lips, her smell stronger than ever. I'll put her to bed at lunchtime, tell myself she needs her rest.

Fit as a fiddle, the police medic said. No harm done. She could go on for years like this.

The pantomime of getting into the car is exhausting. Struggling against the seat belt, her head knocks mine.

'No, no, *no.*' I slap my mother. And just like that, we've crossed a line we'll never get back.

She gawps at me then whimpers. I jab the engine on, my own tears stinging. At the gate, the barrier recalls the metronome's wagging finger. I stare at the guard, begging him to arrest me, save us both.

He waves, we nudge through. Behind us, the barrier's jerky drop is as sudden as the stopped metronome.

We Went There
DEBZ HOBBS-WYATT

We went there he said.

Bone china tea cups, none of them matched. Yellow and white table cloths, red sauce stains. It was raining but the chips were crispy. You must remember.

No, Dad. I don't remember.

How small he looks in the passenger seat. These days I can't help thinking he's been replaced by a little old person I don't recognise.

We went there he said. We sat at the table in the corner, away from the window. Mustn't sit in the window. A coffee machine made hissing sounds. One of the letters was missing.

What was it called?

It was on the corner.

You don't know the name?

There was a wireless playing. A Beatles song. The one they did with someone one else, you know. They sang it together.

I don't know.

Billy someone.

I don't know, Dad.

He's wearing his best suit. I said he didn't need to do that, not the black one, not the one he wore for Mum's funeral.

He said he wanted to wear it, like he understands, like he knows, like he still mourns. But not just for Mum, for who he was. But does he understand what today is?

It's for the best.

He'll like it there.

I reach across and fumble with the dial; there's mist on the windows.

We went there he says and now his fingertips are pressed lightly to the glass and he's making circles. I wonder where he thinks we went. He's been saying it since I told him about Clacton-on-Sea. It's not that far I said, only a couple of hours from London; I'll still be able to come and see you. It's supposed to be a good one. I know someone who went there.

Was it Billy Preston?

Who's Billy Preston?

Who sang with the Beatles on that song?

I don't know, Dad.

You must remember. It was playing on the wireless.

Was I there?

It was the day after they landed on the moon.

I turn and look at him when he says that. He is staring out; he isn't looking at me, and I want to ask him where we went, and how does he know it was the day after they landed on the moon. But I don't say anything. I reach for the button on the radio; fill the car with the poppy up-beats of One Direction. I should've taken some of his CDs out of the box. I could pull over. He likes Sinatra. But he doesn't seem to notice there is music on at all.

We went there he says. She ate ice cream. The woman wore a pinny.

What woman?

The one who brought her the ice cream.

Who had the ice cream?

The little girl.

What little girl?

The one who had ice cream.

Why are all our conversations like this?

What kind of ice cream?

I need to break out of the loop.

The indicator blinks on and off as I pull out into the fast lane; spots of rain hit the window.

Orange.

I didn't know you could get orange ice cream.

I watch the dial on the speedometer nudge seventy-five as I pass an Eddie Stobart truck. Dad is looking at the driver as we speed past. He gives him a thumbs up and then giggles and tells me the driver gave him a thumbs up back and I want to, you know, hug him right there. I'm not a parent but I feel like I am.

The girl's dress he says.

What about it?

Was orange. With patterns in it. Brown swirls. She dripped ice cream on the front.

I look at him. I don't remember going to Clacton.

He's drawn a smiley face on the window, like he used to draw for me on the bathroom mirror. I want to cry. He used to write 'I love you, Iris' in the mist for Mum. I think about the orange dress with the brown swirls and the ice cream dripped on the front.

Dad? Was it me?

Was what you?

The little girl who dripped ice cream on her dress?

I nudge the accelerator.

Where are we going?

Clacton.

I need the toilet.

You just went.

I need to go.

We'll stop at the next place, all right?

Where are we going?

Clacton.

Now he doesn't speak for a bit and One Direction stop singing about 'The Best Song Ever' that's really not the best song ever, and now it's the news. They're saying it's been eight years since Madeline McCann disappeared in Portugal and police are investigating a new lead. I know it's been eight years, Mum died the same week. She kept asking if they'd found her yet. Like she was hanging on until she knew they had. Like it was important to her, so I told her they had; they'd found her. Where? Not far away. Are they in trouble? Who? The people who took her? I don't know, Mum, but she's safe, that's what counts.

Yes she said.

Mum died an hour later.

Mum used to say that's why children should never leave the house; in case something bad happened. They have to leave the house I said. They have to go to school. She said even that's not safe. Men come there. What men come there? Men with guns who shoot children. I wanted to say that never happens but it does. Maybe that's why I was home-schooled until I was twelve. She always thought something bad was going to happen. I think about Madeline McCann as I overtake a fancy sports car; I'm hitting eighty-five; I ought to slow down. I flick on the wipers. I see Dad's eyes move in time to them. He watches them like there's nothing else to look at. I wonder if that's what it's like inside his head.

They're saying there's been a big accident on the A12. But it's going the other way.

We went there he says. Then he goes quiet again and I'm thinking about the rain and the accident on the A12 going the other way. Maybe we did go to Clacton. Mum wasn't always like that; she did used to leave the house. She did used to get out of bed. She never mentioned Clacton though, or holidays. They were both funny about things like that. No holidays. No photo albums. They said they didn't like photos.

I would've been three the year they landed on the moon. Maybe there *was* an orange dress.

The dress, Dad, I say. Did it have an orange bow?

What dress?

The one in the café the little girl was wearing.

Are we going there now?

We're going to Clacton.

We're not supposed to go there.

Why?

In case they come back for her.

Who?

I need the toilet.

We'll stop at the next services.

We used to live near Blackpool; I can't imagine why we'd holiday at Clacton.

The little girl didn't eat her chips.

You mean me, Dad? Was it me?

I think I remember the dress having a bow. I wish he'd use my name, know it was me.

She asked the lady in the pinny for ice cream. She said only if her mummy and daddy said it was okay. She started to cry then, so I said it was okay and asked for a bowl of strawberry ice cream. That's when the little girl said she didn't like strawberry ice cream.

I don't like strawberry ice cream, Dad.

You didn't remember I didn't like strawberry ice cream?

She asked for chocolate ice cream. She spilled it down her dress.

I look at him.

I need the toilet.

Yes, Dad.

When?

Three miles.

Three miles to Clacton?

Three miles to the Little Chef.

Little Chef?

Yeah.

Like a small person who cooks?

No, Dad. I want to laugh then. For a second as I look across at him I swear I see the old Dad, the funny Dad; only this time he doesn't know he's made a joke. It was Dad's idea to let me go to school. Mum had to go away for a bit; the doctors said it was for the best. She was better for a while when she came home; but Dad had to count her pills, make sure she took them. One time she didn't and we found her at the park, riding the roundabout round and round asking the children to push her faster. When Dad stopped it, helped her off, she said my life is like that. Sometimes I want the thoughts to stop.

I know he said. I know, Iris. It's all right.

I was standing there watching and the other children were watching me and I know what they were thinking.

Until I went to school I thought everyone's mum was like that.

I don't like their food, Dad says, and I glance back at him.

Whose food?

I'm doing ninety; the old Dad would have noticed, told me to slow down. But he just stares.

Little Chef. We went there once.

Did we? I don't remember.

It was a Monday.

You remember going to Little Chef on a Monday?

No, Clacton.

I make a note to google the moon landings; find out what day it was.

I don't like the Little Chef.

We're stopping for the toilet, Dad, not to eat.

I want him to look at me, tell me he knows my name and he doesn't blame me for what I'm about to do. I'll be working from home soon and they want David to relocate to the coast, near Clacton, so we'll be even closer. It's for the best.

I turn the wipers onto full speed, look at the speed dial: ninety-five. I wonder what would happen if I pushed it, how fast it would go. I remember the look on Dad's face when I passed my test. Mum stayed in bed. Sometimes I think she missed everything. She was in bed the day I brought David to meet them. I was seventeen, had just started working for the council. I remember them standing in the kitchen, Dad shaking David's hand. He helped us move into our first flat. You will look after her he said to David. I saw his face when he left us there. Same face when we told him a few years later we were moving to London. You could come there, Dad. Move down there.

But your mum, you know …

I knew.

In the end they did move. David persuaded them. They were originally from down south somewhere; they didn't talk about it much. They didn't sound like they were from Blackpool; and nor do I.

I see the sign with the knife and fork. I remember when Dad said how sometimes you do things you shouldn't. What things you shouldn't? You do anything if you love them enough. What things? But all he said was, you should get married, Doris.

Who's Doris?

Huh?

You called me Doris.

I didn't.

It was the first time he called me that.

Have babies. Mum'll like that. She might even come to the wedding.

He never said what things. Mum didn't come to the wedding. We never had a baby.

The doctor said it wasn't David it was me; my eggs, not viable. We could try IVF. I won't leave you, David said, when the IVF failed. Why would you even think that? We could adopt? he said. But I knew he didn't want to raise someone else's child. It's not the same.

The following week we went to the animal shelter.

I'm thinking about slowing down and pulling into the inside lane as we're near the turn-off for the Little Chef when I hear Dad and I turn to look at him. He's making soft whining sounds and his chest is rising and falling in breathy sobs. What, Dad? What's the matter?

I'm sorry.

What for?

I'm trying to get into the slow lane.

Dad, what are you sorry for?

I fist my horn. Dickhead lorry drivers.

I look over – but now he has his hands in his lap and is saying oh dear, oh dear.

I manage to pull into the slow lane. As I do I see the volume of traffic heading the other way; it's slowed right down. Probably the big accident. I hope no one died.

Why are we pulling off?

For the toilet, Dad.

I don't need to go now.

It's all right, Dad. We'll sort it when we get there.

I'm sorry.

Don't cry.

I indicate and pull back into the fast lane, piss off another lorry driver. The traffic going the other way seems to be at a standstill. I'm glad I'm not going that way; although when I look at Dad now, trying to wipe pee off the front of his trousers I think maybe I should turn around. Tell David I couldn't do it. We'll look after him. I know he doesn't want that, but he's my dad.

Where are we going?

Clacton, Dad.

We were there.

Yeah I know.

The day after they landed on the moon.

Yeah you said. Some people say they didn't really go there.

Where?

To the moon.

It was in all the papers.

Yeah, well I'm sure they did go there.

No, I mean it was in all the papers about her.

What are you talking about now, Dad?

The little girl.

I accelerate again; it's raining harder. Dad is watching the wipers again.

I want him to remember my name. I want him to say it.

I wanted to take her back but it was too late.

Who are you talking about?

She looked so much like our little girl.

Me, Dad. That's me. She looked like me? Where was I?

Dead.

What?

The other one was dead.

What other one?

The speed dial is close to a hundred. I bet he's never been to Clacton; he's remembering something on the TV.

Dad, look at me.

He's crying again. I'm sorry he says. She looked like the other one, the one who ran into the road. I was holding on tight, but she …

Shit.

I plug the brake, shit. Shit. SHIT. The traffic up ahead has stopped. I look at the row of red lights in the mist. Instinctively my left arm goes across Dad as the brakes kick in and I try to remember what it said in the *Highway Code* about stopping distance in the rain. Did Dad say someone ran into the road? Another little girl?

Oh my God.

I will the car to stop.

Are we going to die right now?

Jesus.

We're thrown forward.

We miss the car in front by a breath and I look at Dad, I can barely breathe. Even though we were jolted forward he doesn't seem to notice and he's still watching the windscreen wipers sweep across the glass.

The traffic slowly moves forward and we start to move. I don't even know why we stopped. Jesus, there was nearly another accident going this way.

Dad?

Mmm.

What little girl died?

Joanne.

No, Dad. That's me. I'm Joanne. That's me. Jo. Say it, Dad.

He actually remembered my name and I so wanted him to say it, all those times. And now he thinks I'm dead?

I move back into the slow lane, my hands trembling, and I don't know if that's from what he just said or from almost dying on the A12.

Dad.

We went there. The day after they landed on the moon. She looked so much like the other one. We didn't plan it. They weren't looking after her, weren't watching her.

What is he saying now? Dear God what the hell is he saying?

I pull onto the hard shoulder, slow down until we've stopped; the hazard lights blink on and off; I switch off the wipers.

Are we there?

Dad, look at me.

Was it me? Was I the one in the orange dress?

Are we there?

No, Dad, look at me. Please, Dad. What was her name? The one in the orange dress.

Joanne.

I'm Joanne.

We used the same name. Are we in Clacton yet?

What do you mean you used the same name?

Are we there? His hands move to the door and he fumbles with the handle, but it's locked.

Dad?

He pulls at the handle again and now he's crying.

Dad.

We had to go far away.

What was her name, Dad? What was the little girl's name, the one in the orange dress?

But he doesn't need to tell me.

He has called me it enough times.

Dad, was it me in all the newspapers? As I say it, I think about Madeline McCann.

His eyes move to my face and he holds my gaze for a moment, and I think he's going to say it. I think he's going to tell me, and the whole time the rain goes pitter-patter on the window.

Dad? What did you do?

We went there. We bought you ice cream.

He says other things. The rain keeps on pitter-pattering but now all I can hear is one small word: you. He said we bought *you* ice cream.

We went there. Bone china tea cups, none of them matched. Yellow and white tablecloths, red sauce stains. It was raining but the chips were crispy. You must remember.

Yes, Dad, I think I do.

I nudge into the slow lane. I look across at the traffic going the other way, only it's going nowhere. I think about David; about turning around, going back. But what if it's too late? I pump the accelerator, dart into the outside lane. I keep on accelerating until I'm hitting ninety.

Are we there?

We'll be there soon, Dad.

Five
LYNNE E. BLACKWOOD

Five narrow openings Farzhana had carefully left when pulling the blue threads apart to make the embroidered mesh on her *burkha*. They are part of a glistening white criss-crossed pattern of tiny apertures, better to shield her from the outside world. Or so she had been taught. Farzhana tilts her head gently to one side to shift the blue cloth and aligns the silk-grey windows with those opposite. Her gaze pushes through the series of half-open doors towards a freedom denied, blocked by wooden fretwork. In prison; she is in a blue and white embroidered jail with a dissected view, first past the silken mesh covering her face then onto the wall and the windows where the world awaits. Hunched on a low stool, she imagines another life, catches but a fleeting glimpse then adjusts her body in a shiver of resignation. Her hands are clasped under the folds of fine cloth, broken body shrouded beneath billows of blue.

Five narrow windows before her, aligned as tall guards, covered vainly by a broken trellis that allow splintered shafts of daylight to filter through. From the square below arise voices, indistinct. They are men's utterings. Cries and shouts taint the city air with haggling, disputes and greetings. Farzhana observes the dust specks afloat on narrow sun rays. The particles attempt to infiltrate cracks in the worn wood floor. Dancing flecks disappear into the surrounding gloom to settle at random in dim corners and crevices of the room. Some creep into the soles of her feet, mount the soft flesh insidiously, fill her limbs with stillness, infinite sparks of death immobilising her whole body.

Five rays slant across the floor planks to settle on the unique part of her body visible from under the blue cloth. Her immobile feet are encased in velvet slippers gleaming with gold-dust swaying to an invisible melody she cannot join in with. A sunshine jail, she reflects. The sun itself keeps me held down, pins my feet to this dusty floor where I wait. The daily game as she awaits her husband's shrill voice force an angry way up the narrow winding staircase behind her, to pierce the open doorway. Waiting. Always waiting.

Five long years since they came to the city during which her husband's drug addiction had dragged them both from one tenement to another, from poverty to squalor. In this old building, she at least found a reminder of her home in the Afghan countryside. A flat roof where she, as a woman, is forbidden to venture, not even during the hottest summer nights, but to where she creeps in silent velvet slippers when she can go unseen. It is reserved for the men, who sit or lie in dark coolness together, relegating women to the empty room below where Farzhana now sits still and chilled in the early spring afternoon. Leaden tears slip in molten silence down her sunken cheeks. They drop beneath the *burkha* from bowed head onto clasped hands. Farzhana feels them warm her skin for an infinite flash in time, then fade, just as her memories have melted away into an unattainable distance. Short moments, too painful and too joyous to bear at the same time. She holds her body stiff as a corpse, watches the jail pattern of sunrays shift across her slippers in time with the advancing afternoon, punctuated only with traders' cries five floors below.

Five, she had been five when her husband's father had come to the house and she was summoned to sit with them, her mother clutching the small girl's body. Her mother who trembled beneath the *burkha*, who remembered her time as a teacher before the Taliban. This disempowered woman who wondered how her university-educated husband could have become so entrenched in religion to come to this, to sell their only daughter.

My son, Farzhana's future father-in-law asked of her own father, my son will need a wife. He is working in Kabul and is earning good money. He can give a large payment. When can the girl be ready for him?

When she is ten. But I will need a large payment to keep her for your son and another when she goes. I have to keep her for five years. That's a long time. Her father licked his lips. Religion hadn't obscured the desire for gain. Farzhana was sold for money and goats. The money dwindled faster than expected and the goats died. A word spoken was a word given, her father said, despite her now being a burden on his ever-growing and poverty-stricken family.

Five years passed as Farzhana's childhood was transformed into preparation for her female duties. Play with other children around the canals on hot summer days and games of hide-and-seek made way to chores. Then they arrived unannounced one early morning, stating the marriage was imminent and Farzhana should be prepared. The son was on his way from Kabul but could only stay a few days. Farzhana's mother attempted a feeble protest, but in vain, worn out from repeated child-bearing. Five more undernourished children, one for each year that had passed. The family had grown and Farzhana was a worthy income. The second and final payment of the agreement was due and welcomed in a dire time of need as she was taken to her in-law's house for the marriage ceremony. Farzhana was ten years old and traded for the opium that the father-in-law produced, despite the appearance of foreign soldiers who offered seed to plant food crops in exchange. The Taliban paid well for poppy, so Farzhana's father was content.

Five starless nights as her older husband laid rough hands on her body despite her screams, which went unheeded by the family-in-law. The marriage had to be consummated. Then the husband returned to Kabul for business leaving her will broken and malleable in the hands of the in-laws, who used the silent child as a servant. He returned sporadically, and after two miscarriages Farzhana gave birth to their first child at the age of fifteen. The pregnancy and delivery had been an ordeal but she had felt joy, a renewed purpose in her shattered life, vowing never to allow her own daughter to be married so young.

Five years later and she had five children. Girls. Her husband returned at the same time each year in summer to enlarge his family but no son appeared. One day, he arrived to collect her from the farm. We are going to Kabul, he said. The children will go to school, Farzhana exclaimed with relief. An opportunity to save her daughters from becoming child brides. Her husband stared at her with incredulity and contempt. What education do girls need? Better to marry them off as soon as possible. My parents will take care of them and arrange for husbands. You haven't produced a son, so are of no use here. You are coming with me. I need you for my business. He turned his face away, not looking her in the eyes. Farzhana wept.

Five long years without her children and here she crouches five storeys up, beneath the roof where men sit and talk on hot summer nights, above the market place ringing with their strident voices, the braying of donkeys and bleating of sheep. Farzhana listens down the stairwell and hears the voices, quieter now. Outside, spring warmth is reviving blood and street agitation. Men shout, vendors sell wares, arguments and squabbles fill the window frames before her.

Five years of shame, but nothing compared to her husband's disgust and hatred for himself. He needs heroin. Always has. Addiction and a downward spiral of debts had brought them to this miserable tenement. He sells his wife to other men in order to feed his habit. He despises her, but despises himself more. He beats her like a dog.

Farzhana knows the signs, the lull between sentences spoken by the men downstairs. He will climb the stairs and call her to the downstairs room where she will take off her *burkha* in front of those who are buying her body. She will be dressed in enticing western clothes, tight jeans and a top, to display her flesh to drivelling dogs.

Farzhana waits. Thinks of the letter she dictated to a literate friend, a chance encounter when shopping in the market. Come to our charity, the woman had said. We can help you.

No you can't, Farzhana replied. But help my daughters. Take them away from a fate worse than death. The girls would have the chance of freedom and education in an orphanage. Farzhana made arrangements. The girls were to be collected from the village after the charity's payment to her parents-in-law and her letter would be read to them.

The dust dances around the blue cloth as Farzhana hears her husband's steps. He enters. Get down here, now. I've been calling for you to come. I have clients for you. He has had his shoot and slurs over her seated body, hand raised, ready to fall on her blue cloth face. Farzhana slips the gun from under her *burkha* and fires into his exposed ribs.

Five shots slam into her husband's body. He crumples in slow motion. Clouds of dust rise in a wild dance around the body as he smacks the floor with a dull thud. Farzhana watches mesmerised by the blood gushing from his chest. She hears the clients' shouts from downstairs and raises the gun to her forehead, her gaze piercing the windows through the silky-white criss-cross of mesh. The sixth shot rings out. A flawless, circular hole with singed edges appears in the blue cloth, fills the room with the blood red of her freedom.

Death and Biscuits
BEV HADDON

February

Greg needed money, fast. Every morning he bought a scratch card at the station and kept it in his pocket all day, fingering it. Each afternoon, just before he went home, he got out a coin and scratched off the mysterious, shiny silver coating, watching it change to irritating grey flecks of dirt. As financial strategies went, it wasn't much of a plan. But what were the alternatives? Sell his soul to the devil? Bet on Leicester winning the league again?

He sat at his usual table, making a stale ham cob last an hour. Four thirty. Outside the light was fading. Another half hour until he could head home. He stirred his coffee. It wasn't much to look forward to really, having to invent stuff about his day, having to tell Lydia the funny things that had happened in the office. The office. He bit his lip. That bitch from HR had marched him out of the building.

Two weeks he'd spent pretending to go to work. He'd applied for jobs but soon the bills would start coming in, with no money to pay them. It was ridiculous sitting in this café all day, but when he'd tried to tell Lydia his nerve had failed. Her hobbies were shouting and apportioning blame. It was easier to just listen to her telling him about the children: how Jack needed new shoes, how Max had bitten

Lois. Greg would be expected to deal with everything, to tell Max he wasn't supposed to bite people. 'Why?' Max would ask, those eyes, challenging.

Why? Greg didn't have any answers. Why sack him for watching something that happened twenty years ago, two thousand miles away, where everyone looked as though they were enjoying themselves? Even the Alsatian. He shifted his weight, uncomfortable on the wooden chair. And why did anyone came to this God-forsaken café where the only choices of coffee were black or white? There was an old man in the corner. Two teenage girls at the table at the back were having an 'I said, he said' conversation with a lot of swearing. Now and again they glanced around in the hope they were offending someone. The woman who ran the café came when called but otherwise sat in a back room from where Greg could hear the rising cadences of *The Jeremy Kyle Show*. The soothing sound of other peoples' problems.

Someone was speaking to him. He looked up. 'Do you mind if I sit here?' It was the old man, gold-wire spectacles and a greasy-looking sheepskin coat.

'Piss off,' thought Greg, but as he was British, he said, 'Yeah, I mean, no, go ahead.'

The old man set down his cup and saucer. 'I've seen you in here before,' was his opening gambit, 'and I've said to myself, there's a young man with a lot to think about.' A dry, woodwind voice, strong aftershave, long nails, and the yellow-stained fingers of a forty-a-day habit.

Greg made an indeterminate noise. He'd have to find another hopeless run-down café. He wouldn't be coming to this one again.

'A young man with a problem. And maybe I can help.'

Greg summed him up. The old man was a racing tout – maybe he'd give him a hot tip for the 3.50 at Kempton.

'You just need to sell something.'

'Like what?' Greg owned a few shelves of DVDs and a childhood stamp collection.

'Everyone has something to trade.' The old man took a noisy slurp of tea. 'It's like, whaddayoucallit, Facebook. You look at it – you've got more friends than you need. You could lose maybe half of them and you wouldn't notice. You'd be no worse off.'

Greg gave a bitter laugh. 'Unfriending people on Facebook is the least of my problems at the moment.'

'Not friends. Family.' The word seemed to amuse him. He had lots of yellow teeth. 'It's the same principle. Pruning away the dead wood, clearing the weeds.'

There was a pause in the teenage girls' screeching and the old man leaned forward confidentially.

'Everyone has more family than they know what to do with … second cousins, great aunts. They can all be traded. Obviously, the closer to you they are, the more we pay for them. Course, the really big money is for the people you live with. Doesn't have to be blood family either! Mothers-in-law are a *very* popular choice, believe me.'

43

Greg calculated the distance to the door. He pantomimed drinking the last of his coffee and tensed his muscles for a quick getaway. He'd half pushed the chair back when the old man said, 'Ten thousand pounds.'

Greg froze.

'I told you, I can help,' said the old man. 'Get me a packet of custard creams.'

Greg went up to the counter and shouted the woman out of the back room. Maybe he should apply for a job humouring the mentally ill? He sauntered back to the table with another coffee and the packet of biscuits.

'So you're saying you'd give me some money and then just go off and kill cousin Hector?'

'There, you've even decided on a name. No, of course not. I know people who know other people … It's like that pig you're eating.'

(Greg looked down at the remains of his ham cob. It had, he supposed, once been a pig). 'You didn't kill it. The person who sold it to you didn't kill it … There's no connection between you and the chap who did the slaughtering.'

Greg winced at the word 'slaughtering'.

'Ten thousand pounds for someone you haven't seen for years. Maybe you just send them a Christmas card. There! Even saved you a stamp!' Laughter that morphed into a rolling loop of phlegm. The two teenage girls looked around, disgusted.

'You wouldn't get anything out of it. I don't understand.'

'You don't need to understand. You just need to trade. And you've already given me the name. Quick and painless. All you have to do now is to think of the person and say out loud, "I want to trade".'

'I want to trade,' Greg repeated, and, unbidden, there rose up a picture of Hector as he had last seen him, balding, overweight, fussing over something.

He'd done it. He hadn't meant to do it, for God's sake. It was a joke. He was just being kind to an elderly lunatic. It was care in the community! Or perhaps he was being filmed for some dumb Internet site. Best to bluff it out.

'Alright then, that's ten thousand pounds you owe me – plus fifty pence for the biscuits.'

Greg held out his hand.

The old man looked at him speculatively. 'I'll owe you the fifty pence,' he told him. I'll be seeing you, Mr …?'

'Pepper,' said Greg Foster decisively, after casting round desperately for inspiration.

The old man went out and left Greg sitting there. He felt *defiled*. He looked around for a hidden camera and checked in case everyone was looking at him, but people just carried on drinking coffee as if it was a normal afternoon. Greg shook his head and laughed to himself in case he ended up on YouTube. Anyway, it was time he headed home, and he would be happy to see the back of this place. He took out a coin and the scratch card from his pocket. Three seconds later he was racing out of the door to claim his prize, forgetting all about the old man in the shabby café.

Until that evening, when the phone rang.

He was back at the café the next day, sitting there waiting for the old man, a packet of custard creams on the table like some offering to a deity.

'That was quick – ready to trade again?'

'I don't believe this. I didn't give you a surname. I didn't even know his address without looking it up,' Greg whispered. 'What happened to him?'

'Best you don't know anything. After all, you had nothing to do with it – how could you?' A wink.

Greg stirred his coffee. Hector's sister had told Greg how she had found him, lying on the ground. It seemed he had leaned backwards out of his bedroom window, overbalanced and fallen. There was a dishcloth on the ground – she thought he'd been trying to wipe away some cobwebs. Leaned too far. Greg had pressed her for the time of death, hoping it was before four thirty. It wasn't. He'd had a bad night; when he finally slept, his dreams were all of defenestration and spiders.

'Word of advice, once you have decided to trade, keep out of the way, especially if they have left you anything in their will. Also, I'm told, it can be distressing.' The old man chuckled at the very idea. 'Next time you want to trade …'

('I won't,' said Greg. 'Ever.')

'… Just think of the person, say it out loud.'

('I won't,' said Greg. 'Ever.')

Drops of tea hung from the old man's moustache.

'No need for us to meet again. Payment won't be direct – buy some more scratch cards, do the lottery – maybe an accumulator bet on the gee-gees … Put something on the 3.50 at Kempton!'

March

Greg sidled in at the back, half expecting everyone to turn around and the corpse to sit up and point at him. He had to know, for sure, that Hector was really dead – that this was not some enormous, complicated practical joke. But it was a normal funeral. People said nice things about Hector, then talked about football and the weather, and Greg gradually calmed down. He was impressed that he was able to give his considered opinion on City's chances in the league. He felt it showed a certain moral courage to attend the funeral of someone he had almost certainly not murdered. Because it was nonsense – it had to be. Just one crazy old man and a series of coincidences. After all, what was the alternative? Something in red tights with a toasting fork?

Greg said hello to his Great Aunt Edith at the funeral. She'd always been so active, so independent, but here she was, stuck in a wheelchair with only one good arm. People fussed over her, bringing her cups of tea, and you could see that she hated it. Poor Great Aunt Edith. She didn't want to be a burden. She'd had enough.

May

He carried on applying for jobs (he'd told Lydia he'd been made redundant) but they weren't interested when they saw he'd been sacked. In between worrying about money, he kept thinking about Great Aunt Edith. How she had been at the funeral. It bothered him, the state she was in, dependent on carers to get her out of bed and take her to the toilet.

'Don't get old!' she'd said at the funeral, and he had laughed. Life was so unfair. His eyes filled at the thought of how she had ended up. If only he could do something about it …

June

'Mr Foster, Greg, (can I call you Greg?) I can see how hard it has been for you losing your aunt, how grief-stricken you are.'

Greg was surprised. Was he grief stricken? It was true that Great Aunt Edith had been frequently in his thoughts, which is why, after arranging and paying for the funeral (it was the least he could do) he had asked if he could have a few minutes with her to say goodbye.

'I really don't think that's a good idea …' said the girl in the funeral parlour, her eyes wide as she looked around desperately for help. A grey-haired woman in a grey suit had taken his arm and steered him to a comfy grey sofa.

'The thing is, your aunt – she was wartime generation, wasn't she? The sort of person who would have carried on regardless. She would have wanted you to just get on with your life, and not mourn for her – after all, she was a good age, wasn't she?'

'Eighty-eight,' said Greg. He was proud that he knew that.

'… And she would have wanted you to remember the good times – she would have wanted you to remember her as she was, getting the kettle on, bustling, busy. Not …'

'You're right,' said Greg. They all waved him goodbye.

It was a lovely funeral. Everyone said so. When it was time to file out of the crematorium, Greg patted the coffin affectionately. The lid was firmly nailed down.

July

Greg slouched in the draughty church waiting for Uncle Phil's funeral to kick off. He picked up the service leaflet and studied it with a jaundiced eye. When the coffin came in, Greg glared at it and grudgingly stood up. He mimed 'Abide With Me'. An hour of his life he'd never get back.

Uncle Phil had not been traded.

September

Greg had stopped applying for jobs. He thought he might set up in business on his own, perhaps as some sort of financial consultant. He had taken up genealogy as a hobby. He had lots of free time to research his great-grandparents and trace their descendants. He was pleased to find members of his family he hadn't even known existed! Although he was disappointed that some of them were already dead.

December

Coming away from his grandmother's sister's daughter's husband's funeral, Greg was cut up by his second cousin Tyrone driving a black Audi A3. Tyrone gave him an ironic wave and a toot of his horn. Greg had traded him before they reached the next set of lights.

February

Greg was at the café waiting for it to open. When it did, he swept up all the biscuits into a pile, paid and dumped them on a table.

The old man came in two minutes later, shouted a cheery greeting to the café owner and then took forever ordering a pot of tea. He came over to sit with his young friend.

'You look unhappy.'

'You killed him.'

'You wanted to trade – we traded.'

Greg closed his eyes. That night in Spain. The holiday that had descended into farce. Max didn't like anything –

the food, the heat, the villa – 'Why couldn't they get Wi-Fi? Why couldn't they go home?' Max had hit Lois and Greg had hit Max, hard, but the boy had just stared back up at him. And then he had thought (only thought) 'I wish I could trade *you*.' The thought had vanished as fast as it came. He hadn't said anything; maybe his lips had moved. Everyone had calmed down and gone to bed. He was almost sure he hadn't said it out loud.

When Greg got up the next morning there was a packet of custard creams in the kitchen and he had thrown them at the wall in panic. Lydia had looked at him as if he was insane. She had found a shop that ex-pats used – it sold English food, cornflakes, Marmite, and she'd bought everything in the hope there was something that Max would condescend to eat. Greg wasn't reassured; he had stuck close to him, alert to every danger. They were supposed to be driving to a new beach that afternoon but Greg had vetoed that. They stayed in the villa, sunbathing around the pool. But, of course, Max was bored; within ten minutes he had lobbed Lois's Mr Elephant into the middle of the pool. It sank.

'Max, you get that out at once!' yelled Lydia from inside, hearing the wails.

When Max jumped in, Greg had jumped in with him. When Max stayed under the water, Greg had grabbed a breath and squatted down, panicking as he saw the boy's toe was caught in one of the drains. He tried to free him, then tried to give his breath to his son but Max had blindly hit out at him until his body went limp. The holiday company had admitted liability and promised a substantial cheque; generous for a child he had struggled to love.

Pruning away the dead wood.

'You told me it would be quick and painless,' he blurted out.

'No, no, I said trading is quick and painless, for *you*.'

The old man ripped open packets of sugar, taking his time. 'So how are things at home?'

Greg's hands curled into fists.

'Quieter? More peaceful?'

Yes, was the answer. Lois and Jack had been afraid of Max. It didn't make it right.

'I never want anything to do with you again. It's over. When I get the cheque it's going to charity.'

The old man picked a seed out of one his teeth. 'Very noble, I'm sure. And I'm sure that your wife *fully* supports your decision.'

Lydia had taken it better than he had. She hadn't watched Max die. She had even talked about what they should do when they got the compensation cheque, taking no notice of Greg's haggard expression. She thought they should extend the house, add a games room, a home cinema, maybe even a Jacuzzi. He hadn't bothered to listen. It wasn't happening. The money was going to help orphaned refugees. Some good would come from Max's death.

'You're the devil,' he said flatly. 'Buying my soul on H.P.'

The old man snorted. 'The things you say. You should be on the telly.'

'It's over,' said Greg again.

The old man shrugged. 'I have other clients. Goodbye, Mr Pepper.'

Greg let himself in to the house and headed for the kitchen. When he clicked the kettle on there was a flash and he woke up on the floor, spitting out blood and vomit. He tried to say 'Help me' although his teeth and tongue seemed to be in the wrong places, but it seemed that no one understood him as no help was forthcoming. He wondered how long it would take him to die. The last thing he heard was someone saying something about a Jacuzzi.

Where to Stay, What to Do
LINDSEY FAIRWEATHER

'This is it,' she said, turning a key in the massive green door. A smaller door within it swung open and she stepped through, holding it open for him.

They entered the dark stairwell and a dim light snapped on overhead. It was surprisingly cool inside, and the sweat that had developed on Sam's forehead suddenly chilled him.

He kept a hand on the rail as they climbed the curving staircase. Helen's linen dress swished a little as they went up. She'd been here for a week already, doing some intensive language training. 'You can come out when I do,' she'd said, 'but for the first week at least, it's supposed to be immersion, so…'

That was all right. He'd stayed in London, drinking pints with friends in shabby pubs and taking walks along the Thames. But without Helen, London seemed empty. It was summer; since he was a teacher, he was suddenly free, blinking in the intermittent sunshine with whole days ready to unspool at his feet. Summer days were always long, and they melted into each other. During the past few summers, he rarely knew what day of the week it was until he woke to find Helen still sleeping beside him. Then he knew it was Saturday.

Now their footsteps echoed in the stairwell. He could feel his heart throbbing and he wondered if he was excited or exhausted or both. When they'd huffed up three floors, she stopped and produced another smaller key.

'Wilkommen,' she said as she pushed open the door and went inside. Daylight poured into the hallway and he stood there for a moment, dazzled. She was already calling to him from somewhere deep in the flat. He stepped over the threshold.

#

Soon after Helen landed this job, he had bought and read three Vienna travel books, cover to cover. They prepared him for splendor. The cakes were beautiful, the fondant sculpted just so, the kaffee mit schlagobers rich and decadent. The buildings were breathtaking, the parks pristine. It was a Disney-perfect kingdom, the books insisted.

'And you get to live there,' his mother had said. 'Put Helen on so I can congratulate her.'

With three months to go before the move, he asked to see the Post report, a twenty-page internal document about the Embassy and the city. He read about popular neighborhoods, places to eat, tipping customs. He read that he would be entitled to German lessons once they arrived in Vienna.

'We'll move into my predecessor's place,' Helen said. 'It's a block from the Belvedere Palace.'

'The Kiss,' he said.

'What?'

'The Palace is a gallery now, with a bunch of Klimt paintings. 'The Kiss' is there. You know the one. Gold leaf, picnic blanket.'

'Sounds romantic,' she said, grabbing the report, throwing it over her shoulder, unbuckling his belt.

It was all very lucky, very fortunate, yes.

He downloaded some apps and tried to learn German but it was a choppy, ugly, unmemorable language for him. The words wouldn't stick. But he didn't say anything, because Helen's best work friend and his fiancee were heading to Islamabad soon. His own anxiety seemed klein against that. Klein—'small'—a word he'd worn on the waistband of his underwear, for goodness sake. What a humiliating joke.

So they were going, and that was that.

'We need to buy some boxes,' Sam said, looking at their bookshelves after takeout curry one evening.

'You're sweet.' She squinted at him to see if it was a joke. 'Honey, the movers are coming. They'll do it all.'

'Right,' he said. It was as if the gears of some great machine were turning and he was a cog separate from it all, unheeded and entirely unnecessary. Useless parts eventually found their way to the trash, he knew, bending to kiss Helen's shoulder.

#

The summer they moved, Vienna was hot. He woke up hot, was hot all day, and at night the sheets stuck to his body. Helen didn't seem to mind it, but she had the cool office to sit in, and her commute was negligible. Sometimes Sam walked to the Ringstrassen Gallerien mall just to sit in the cool air. Fancy watches and fur coats flanked the marbled hallways. Old Austrian women shopped there, and they were so different from the old women he'd grown up with—these women adhered to a frigid formality he did not understand. Sometimes as he sat on a bench or waited in line at the grocery store, they shook their heads and tutted at him. He never learned why.

October came, fast and rainy. Their heavy baggage arrived at last and he spent two days unpacking their things: clothes, kitchen gadgets, framed photographs of their travels. One day he arranged their books by color, and then by genre, and then finally put them on a pile on the floor and alphabetized them on the shelves. It took hours, which annoyed him, but then again, he had hours, which annoyed him even more.

He had been valedictorian in high school, and magna cum laude in college. Here he didn't even know how to say what he'd become. What was German for 'nothing'?

He bought a PlayStation.

'Learn German,' Helen said one night after dinner. 'Or get a job.'

In the gray mornings, he scoured online job boards for teaching or tutoring work. He wrote emails in English. Dear Sir or Madam. I attach my CV.

Replies were rare, and the ones that did come in asked him if he had the right to work. The answer was 'not yet' because he and Helen were not yet married and he had no hope of a European passport till they were. 'It is with sincere regret,' the faceless secretaries wrote to him. He could imagine pearls tapping collarbones as they typed.

One Monday morning, when he pulled the door shut and stepped onto the rain-slicked street, he considered that on this date in three years they would be living somewhere new. It was the nature of her job. It could be some bright desert place, or somewhere snowy and mountainous. He didn't know which he'd prefer.

He was late for his lesson. He ran for the tram and sat on one of the wooden benches. As the tram started to move, he saw a large green parrot fly past the window. He twisted his neck to look back at it but it was gone. What could it be doing here, so far from what must be home?

Today he and his fellow students would introduce themselves to each other again. His class was full of teenage Turkish girls. A couple of them showed up only half the time, and they giggled their way through the exercises.

'They're here because of the settlement requirement,' an English woman whispered when she saw him staring. 'They need to come to at least half the sessions.'

'Oh.'

One of the Turkish girls was particularly pretty, so pretty that he forgave her silliness when they were partnered together for speaking exercises. Her eyeliner was always just so, her lips cherry red. Today they were talking about family. 'Ich bin geheiratet,' she said. I'm married.

He remembered their conversation from last week. 'Ich habe siebzehn yahre.' I'm seventeen.

He reached for a word, but he had so few German words, and all of them were wrong now; it was like reaching a bare arm into a wasp's nest and expecting to find honey there. 'Wünderbar,' he said.

After four weeks, his entitlement to language classes ran out. He could pay for more, but with what money? He didn't want to ask Helen.

He held the door for the pretty Turkish girl as she left the school, completion certificate in hand. She walked through the door without glancing at him.

They hadn't learned much in the class. He could list fruits, vegetables, basic autobiographical information, the numbers one to twenty... and he knew how to say Gemütlichkeit — 'cosiness' — which didn't seem particularly handy, but, seeing as winter was on the way, he kept it in his pocket like a lighter, just in case.

His classmates were scattering now, the English woman giving him a little wave as she crossed the road and disappeared into a shop.

He went to a cafe and tried to read a newspaper, but after a few minutes of staring at the words without comprehending them, he paid the grumpy waiter and left.

He was in the bathroom when he heard Helen unlock the front door.

'Hi honey,' he called.

When he came into the kitchen, drying his hands on his jeans, he found her peering into the Dutch oven. She took off her glasses, which had gone opaque in the steam. 'I thought you were going to make a tagine,' she said.

'Not today,' he said, but it was true. They were having pork chops now, because at the meat counter, he could not remember any appropriate words to say, and wound up panicking, pressing a finger to the cold glass and then raising two fingers. He had wanted lamb shoulder. All he could remember to say was 'Danke', though he wasn't grateful at all. He gave up, retraced his steps through the long fluorescent aisles and put back the couscous, the apricots, the saffron. After paying the man at the till, he shoved the unfamiliar change in his pocket and finally felt his cheeks burn.

'What did you do today?' she asked as they sat down to eat.

'Not much. It was fine.'

'Good.'

Ask me again, he thinks, suddenly, desperately. Ask me once more and I'll tell you.

He had not spoken to anyone for five hours, except for that 'Danke', and now the pork was dry and he couldn't think of anything to say.

He wanted to grab her, carry her to bed, because he had chosen her, had meant to choose her. He could still have one thing today that he'd chosen.

'I'm tired,' she said, pushing her plate toward him. She'd left half the food behind. 'Let's just watch a little TV and go to bed.'

'Sure.'

He did the dishes while she sat on the couch and Skyped her mom. More wedding planning.

He scooped the remaining pork into a tupperware for her lunch tomorrow. They brushed their teeth side-by-side and then Helen fell asleep right away. Behind the heavy curtains, the white, sculpted city slept too. 'Ich bin geheiratet,' he whispered, just testing it out in the dark.

The weekend crawled toward them, and Saturday finally came, bright and expectant. Helen made some cheese sandwiches and they bought small, strong coffees from a stand on the corner. They wandered down the stairs and out the door-within-a-door.

'The 1 Tram used to go in a circle,' he said, stepping onto the street. 'The 2 did, too, in the other direction. My German teacher told me.'

'And—?'

'And nothing. That's all I got.'

'Okay.' She was staring out the window. Not at him. Never at him anymore.

As the days shortened, he walked around the ring road and walked the cobbled streets of the old town. The buildings were beautiful, though too similar to be of much interest after a while.

The soles of his shoes wore down fast on the cobbles; replacing them was costly but what could he do? The cobbler near the station smoked all day, clouding his tiny glass shop. He smiled at Sam with incongruously white teeth. When Sam picked up his shoes—'Vielen Dank,' he remembered to say—they stank like cigarettes for weeks.

Spring came. Helen bought a pink checkered dirndl and wore it like the locals, without irony, to a local vineyard in the foothills of the Alps. He bought lederhosen and modeled them in the hallway of their apartment.

'I feel like a dick,' he said.

'No, they're sweet,' Helen insisted, snapping a photo and posting it to Facebook before he could stop her.

He found a job teaching English to businessmen. It was just two hours a day, in the late afternoon, and paid cash. In the evenings and weekends, they followed the suggestions in their travel guide. They queued at Figlmueller and ate schnitzel bigger than the dinner plate it was served on. Another time, they sat in the fading light at a picnic table beside a vineyard; they drank young white wine while men in suits clinked glasses nearby. Sam patted his pocket, hoping he'd left a crumpled bill in it. 'Don't worry,' Helen said, but he saw the men and he did.

When Helen suddenly retched near Karlsplatz as a horse and carriage went by, Sam knew she was pregnant. They bought a test from an old-fashioned pharmacy, just to be sure. Its wooden shelves were lined with glass bottles. My life is over, Sam thought, waiting to pay. He hadn't even had the chance to enjoy his last bit of innocence. Now it was gone. You can't un-ring the bell, his childhood priest used to say.

Helen peed on the plastic stick when they got home while Sam stood outside the bathroom door. 'You can come in now,' she said. Her face was very white. The test line showed up within seconds, solid and pink. Sam's jaw was tight as they waited the requisite few minutes, Helen perched on the side of the tub while he sat on the lid of the toilet.

'Just one line—not pregnant then,' Sam said, his heart trilling.

'No,' she said. 'Look.'

A faint second line had appeared. 'But that's barely there,' he said.

'It's there.' Her voice was flat. 'You can't be a little bit pregnant.'

Two parallel lines now: 'pause', the test seemed to say. He desperately wanted to.

'No skiing for you, I guess,' Sam said, and immediately regretted it and wanted to rewind the last few minutes, the last few weeks.

They booked a flight to Detroit for Easter. Helen had to get a letter from her doctor to allow her to travel, since she was into her seventh month.

'Tickets are so expensive,' she said over his shoulder while he typed his credit card number. But they had had this conversation before, and that was the deal. He was so far away, so much of the time.

She spent the flight clutching an airsickness bag. He realised there was nothing he could do to help, so patted her back once and turned on a violent movie. She hated those so they never went to them together; this was his only chance.

His parents met them at the airport and they told Helen she was glowing—a flat-out lie, Sam thought, looking at her still-greenish face.

They slept side-by-side on his childhood bed, surrounded by his old bowling trophies and posters of baseball players, the corners now curling up and away from the wall.

'So will the baby be Austrian?' his mom asked over blueberry pancakes the next morning. She was already ill; her veins throbbed thin and blue at her temples and during her violent bouts of post-Chemo vomiting, blood vessels had burst like little fireworks on her cheeks.

'No. British and American,' he said. There would be a lot of paperwork to do, he realised, lots of sitting in crowded consulates with nervous applicants and overworked bureaucrats. Chipped plastic chairs and little slips of paper with numbers on them. And flights would be so much more expensive now—would Helen insist they visit less often?

Helen was shoveling pancake wedges into her mouth. His head began to throb.

'Well, that's good,' his father said, cutting his omelet. 'So many opportunities.'

That night, with Helen snoring beside him in bed, a pillow beneath her belly and another between her knees, he felt his life sliding into focus, slowly, slowly, the bits of it aligning.

He crept downstairs and saw two Easter baskets on the table. His mother still tried to make things magical when he knew damn well by now that nothing was. He found some bunny-shaped marshmallows in one of the baskets, dusted with neon yellow sugar. He ripped open the packet and ate them all, one by one, methodically and without joy.

The rest of the week passed quickly. They played cards at night, rain drumming on the roof of the screened-in porch. They ate processed foods. He slept deeply, dreamlessly. At the airport, he was too numb to cry when he hugged his mother goodbye. I'll never see you again, he thought.

Helen threw up three times on the flight back to Vienna. He could not see the Atlantic below them in the darkness.

Numbness closed over him like a fist as they sped through the foreshortening night.

They landed Sunday morning, unpacked their suitcases in silence, and put a frozen pizza in the oven. Helen took an afternoon nap and they went to bed early, with a dry kiss. The next morning, the firm click of the door behind her announced another five days of loneliness.

Sam made himself a coffee and tried to read a book. He was disoriented, jet-lagged. He packed a sandwich and his guidebook and hailed a tram outside the flat.

He rode the 1 Tram to the end of the line. The route was no longer a circle; it took him far away, just as he hoped. He stepped down onto the platform. Birds were singing in the vineyards. He thought about hailing a cab and going to the airport—it wouldn't take long, now that he was out of town. It would be so easy.

But as he stood there at the tram stop he knew with terrible certainty that he would return; he would walk through the door, up the stairs, toward the light and the voice welcoming him to a place that would never be home.

Suicide Vending Machine
THOMAS WELSH

Good morning, sir. I see from my paperwork that you have a budget of ten thousand dollars, but I'm pleased to tell you that you can benefit from our 'recommend a friend' discount scheme. Yes, sir, it's another three thousand, and you should certainly thank them the next time you see them. Or perhaps allow us to send them a message of thanks on your behalf?

I am glad you asked! You absolutely can make a referral too. Don't worry; I'll remind you when we finalise our documentation. Just the name and location is all we need. We will pick them up.

All right then, let's begin!

Now, of course I am the salesman, but I am also a guide, because these machines sell themselves. After all, why would you skimp on the last thing you'll ever buy? The Life Transition Machines start at one thousand dollars, but we recommend you consider our 'best value' package. We have a range of finance options available.

I already know what your next question will be. And yes, for the sake of authenticity, the machines really do take coins. We offer large-denomination, special-run tokens. You wouldn't want to be standing here all day, would you? We find that most of our customers don't want to spend their final hours depositing thousands of coins into a slot. That would be neither authentic nor practical.

Ah, I see you eying up the mid-range options. Great for a man on a budget who doesn't want to compromise on quality. The dark blue machine to your right may be of interest. As you can see, there are two main receptacles, one for each arm. You slide your hands inside – after you've deposited your payment of course – and the machine will bleep twice to let you know it's ready. Stainless steel bracelets will secure your wrists in place, locking you at the exact angle necessary for a clean, precise procedure. The incision takes place in one... let me just check the specs in my documentation here... yes, it takes place in 'one one-thousandth of a second', severing both arterial veins with a single nanometre-sharp edge. That's the real genius of this particular machine: a single motion so fast and fluid that you won't feel a thing.

From there, you can either pull your wrists free – the locking mechanism will release automatically after the incision – or you can lean your weight on the moulded Corinthian leather armrests. We find some of our customers are interested in the aesthetic side and want to see the results of the machine's work, while others are happy for the residual mess to stay inside. We either mop up afterwards, or inside the machine a vacuum chamber means you won't see a drop. Of course, as with all procedures that cut the wrists, we don't cross the street, we go up the highway.

Vertical cuts are far more effective at severing the appropriate arteries than horizontal.

No? I see that perhaps this one is not for you, but please follow me! I have something far more suited to your tastes.

Let's see, let's see... Yes, along this way please. Ah, here we are! Now this machine in the green is actually a little cheaper. Many customers are put off by the nature of its operation, but discerning individuals like yourself might be able to handle it. It's not for everyone, but if you're up for a bit more of a challenge in your transition from this life to the next, this is a good choice. Shall I tell you more?

I know it looks a little more intimidating, but its operation is both simple and effective. You put your head through this space here. As you can see, there are handholds at either side so you can steady yourself. Now, as you put your head inside this gap, the metal actuators release. You see the black band here? This is a three-inch-diameter vulcanised rubber with a tensile strength of... let me quickly check... yes, 'half a tonne'. The metal hands release this band and it snuggly compresses the neck. You see the sophistication of this design? The metal hands hold it open wide enough for your head to fit comfortably through, but with a taut radius much smaller than the thinnest neck, this band is absolutely effective one hundred per cent of the time.

What's that? No, not suffocate. The mechanism of transition is down to the blood flow being cut off rather than the air. Yes, it is quite quick.

Are you interested in suffocation? Please, sir, I am only asking! Of course we can skip over those machines. If it's not to your taste, I recommend you ignore the yellow one. Yes it laminates. You, sir… it laminates you.

Certainly I could tell you about the white machine. Yes, it is quite pricey, but we are very proud of it. Cutting edge, certainly, but also refined and classic. You see the smooth bezel down the side? Ivory inlays. Ultra HD display screen. I agree, it is quite difficult to identify exactly what it does just by looking at it. The mechanism in this machine is very small. You see this panel here? It looks like a key slot, but actually, if you push your finger inside – no, sir, don't do that right now – well, if you place your finger in here a micro-syringe will push through the fur coating and deposit a tiny dosage of our secret formula into the tip of your finger. Not intravenous, this formula doesn't need to go directly into your veins. Paralysis at first. Look down, sir, you see the mat on the floor? Padded and shock absorbent. It's a little like a very peaceful sleep. Yes, sir, a forever sleep.

Perhaps we could look at the red machine. It's far closer to your budget and offers a – no, sir, come over here please! I'm afraid that area is off-limits. What is it? Why, sir, that isn't one of our machines! That's the door. Well, yes, it's an entrance, but it's not also an exit. Not unless you have the cancellation fee at hand. Fifteen thousand. No, sir, financing is not available for that option.

Would you like to see the blue machine again?

Metropolis
MARIANNE WHITING

We were all poor in the Berlin tenements where I lived. Some had been poor before the Great War as well; others had been better off then. Not that any of us children who crowded the potholed street remembered much about the war. I was two when it ended. Memories came second-hand in sad stories told by mothers and grandmothers, but not by the men, they didn't talk much. We played outside in the summer-dust, in the autumn-puddles and in the winter-snow. We scavenged in dustbins and rubbish heaps. The country had been at peace for six years but we were still hungry.

When a shiny black limousine pulled up at the end of the street we raced each other to get there first, to get close enough to touch. Most of us had never seen a real car before, certainly not in this area. Two men got out. They wore good coats open over proper suits and their shoes looked brand new. They didn't go anywhere. They just stood there looking at us.

'These look suitably skinny and hungry. We could take them all.'

'We almost have enough already. Berlin seems full of scrawny urchins. I never imagined it would be like this. It's been quite an eye-opener. Ah, and here come the adults. We should be able to use some of them too.' Men, back early from job-hunting, were drifting closer, hands in pockets, dejected shoulders hunched. From under the peaks of cloth caps their eyes were fixed on the cigarettes in the gloved hands of the strangers. When the fag-ends were thrown away they would be snatched up by a child almost before hitting the ground, and a father or elder brother would be happy.

When the strangers finally spoke to us we couldn't believe our luck. They offered us work. They were making a film and needed what they called 'extras' – those are people who are in a film to make up the numbers. That suited us just fine. We didn't even have to fight for this work, they wanted us all. Well, except for the two fat children from the house at the end of the road whose father drove the number 15 tram and who were fed three meals every day. It was the only time I can remember that I didn't envy them. We were going to get food and money and be in a film. It seemed too good to be true. I had never seen a film, but Mother told me they were like magic photographs that moved.

The men had to shave off their hair and look like prisoners.

'At least I know about that,' said Dad. He'd been a prisoner of war for three years. We had a proper meal that evening, potatoes and cabbage. I was so happy I couldn't sleep.

'I can't let you go in those shoes,' said my mother. 'People will think you're not cared for.' I looked down at my leather boots. The holes in the soles didn't show and I kept putting bits of cardboard or newspaper inside to keep the worst of the mud out. But there was no disguising the open toes, which were necessary as my feet had grown too large to fit inside. It got a bit cold in the winter but most of the time it didn't bother me. Plenty of children had holes in their shoes where we lived. But this was different. I was going to work. My mother let me wear her shoes. We stuffed the toes with old rags and I stumbled round our one room practising walking without tripping myself up.

A truck came to pick up the children. The grown-ups had to make their own way to the studios. When we arrived, there were hundreds of us, all from different parts of the city. The only thing we all had in common was that we were thin and looked hungry. A tall man in a suit came and looked down at us from a platform. I could only see one of his eyes, the other was covered by a lens.

'That's Herr Lang, the director,' said a boy next to me.

'Has he only got one eye?'

'That's a monocle. It's like glasses but for one eye. He wears it all the time.'

'In bed too?'

'Don't ask silly questions.'

'But does he?' The boy didn't answer but turned to speak to someone else. I felt a bit scared of Herr Lang. But I decided that if I ever got a chance I would ask him if he did wear his monocle in bed. I really wanted to know.

I never got close enough to speak to Herr Lang so I never found out. I got closer to Brigitte Helm. She was beautiful, with curly blonde hair and dark red lips. Us children jostled to try to get next to her and smell her perfume. I was usually pushed out of the way by the bigger children. Herr Lang and the cameraman sat on platforms suspended above us and every now and then Herr Lang would shout at the camera to swoop in and film someone close up. The huge metal arm of the crane moved above our heads until the cameraman was satisfied. It frightened me at first, but I got used to it and stopped turning my head to watch the camera instead of in front as I had been told to. Herr Lang was a stickler and would make us do the same thing many times, often till late into the night. That was boring and tiring, but most of the time it didn't matter, not until we got to the flood.

In the film the underground city was flooded and Brigitte Helm saved all the children from drowning. She looked so brave I could quite imagine her doing that in real life too. We had to wade through water that became deeper and deeper before she got us out to safety. It didn't do Mother's shoes much good and I was very worried the first time I returned home with them soaking wet. Mother didn't get angry about it though. Every evening she took out the rags and hung them to dry, and the shoes too. In the morning I stuffed the rags back in. The shoes weren't always dry, but that made little difference because I was soon standing in freezing water again thinking about the money I was earning and the food we were able to buy with it.

We may have been thin, hungry children, but we were tough. Even so, the long hours immersed in cold water, sometimes up to our thighs, took its toll, and sneezing and sniffling became commonplace. I caught it too, but while most of the others got better I got worse. My head ached, I had a sore throat and I shivered constantly. I was very tired and had to force myself out of bed and ready for the truck in the morning. But I kept going. Until one day I fainted and fell face first into the dirty water. The shock brought me back and the other children helped me to my feet. Herr Lang must have seen, because he bellowed: 'Fräulein Helm, pick up that girl and carry her for the last stretch. Ah, but this is fantastic! Such realism!' Brigitte Helm looked angry, but nobody argued with Herr Lang, so the great star made her way to me and clasped me to her fine dress with the nice lace collar. I breathed in the delicious scent of her perfume and, delirious in every sense of the word, I didn't mind at all when I had to do it over and over again. Six times I dived into the water and was picked up by Brigitte Helm before Herr Lang was satisfied. I was so enthralled I didn't even notice that I had lost my mother's shoes.

Two of the boys from our street made sure I got on the truck and took me home that evening. It was two days before I woke up and cried out in a panic about having missed work and having lost Mother's shoes. I wasn't allowed to go back to the studio. Mother cried and said she shouldn't have let me go once I caught the cold.

I recovered from my illness, Father's hair grew out again and there was just enough money from what he and I earned on the film to buy Mother a pair of second-hand shoes. My old boots with the toes cut open had to last another winter until Father found work again. The film was called *Metropolis*. I never saw it. We didn't have money for cinema. The two fat children whose father drove the number 15 tram did. They said they never saw me in it. They said it was crap anyway.

Real Love (Makes Your Lungs Burn)
JACK WEDGBURY

Mick the Knife pulled the pickup around the back, parking it off the street. He left the engine running. He looked out at the long line of red-brick terraced houses. The sun hung over them now, light glinting off the slate roofs. Behind, the trees stretched their branches high above, clawing at the sky.

Hers was the middle house. He pressed the horn and saw Honey come to the window. She signalled 'two minutes'. His foot tapped as he waited.

She walked out the back door and down the path, wearing a flannel shirt and Chelsea boots. She came to the open passenger-side window and leaned in.

'You look *smart*,' she said. 'Gonna try it on with the judge?'

'Fuck off,' he said.

She laughed. 'Whose truck is this?'

'It's mine, baby. Get in.'

She stepped back and looked again. 'Isn't it Peter Jarrod's – the farmer?'

'Alright, I'm borrowin' it. Come on, get in, Honey.'

'He ain't gonna like it, Mickey. I heard he keeps a gun behind the seat.'

'Does he fuck.'

'Did you check?'

'No. I'm not messin', Honey. *Get in*.'

'Alright, mardy,' she said, opening the door and sliding into the seat.

His foot was tapping again.

'What's going on?' she said.

'We ain't goin'.'

'Why not?'

'I've been thinkin' about what you said the other day. How you've never been to the beach. I wanna take you.'

'When?'

'Now.'

She looked at his hands. He was spinning the rings around his fingers.

She placed her hand on the back of his neck. 'What's *really* going on?'

He looked out of the window, at the trees behind her house. 'It ain't gonna be a slap on the wrist this time, Honey,' he said, quietly. 'I'm lookin' at years.'

'You don't know that for sure.'

'You saw the way they looked at me! It ain't gonna be like last time.'

'Mickey… You'll make it worse if you skip bail.'

'Baby, I don't want to go to prison.'

'I know. I don't want you to either. But you'll be okay.'

'It's not that—' His eyes filled suddenly. He turned away.

There was a silence. Honey stroked the back of his neck. He pressed his buttoned shirt to his eyes. He cleared his throat. When he turned back, he didn't look at her, but instead down at his hand, on her thigh.

'I don't wanna be without you,' he said.

She looked at him. His dark brow was drawn down, his eyes edged in pink. He looked up. She smiled.

'What?' he said.

'You.'

She leaned in, touching her forehead to his.

'I just need a little longer,' he said. 'Let's get away for a while.'

'Really?'

'Why not?'

'We don't have any money.'

'We'll get some.'

'And then?'

'Maybe it will cool off, or maybe we'll just keep goin'.' He squeezed her thigh. 'It's just me and you, Honey. There's a whole world out there to get lost in.'

He looked at her. She looked back at the house, and then at him.

She lifted his hand and kissed it. 'Let me get my jacket.'

The drive out of town was open roads and cigarettes. The sun rose and rose, and the landscape changed from grey to green and gold. Fields of wheat swayed in the breeze at the roadside. The air smelt clean, like dry grass. Behind them, the small town reduced to nothingness. Mick checked the rear-view regularly, as though to assure himself. The further they drove, the lighter he felt. The tarmac stretched out endlessly before them, winding and twisting on forever.

Honey wound the window down and let her arm hang, wriggling her fingers against the breeze. Her shirt flapped against her skin. The wind whipped her bleach-blonde hair up around her face. Fractured light cut in through the window – a soft, golden light that made her skin glow. She closed her eyes and tilted her face up to the sunshine. She was iridescent. Mick was hardly watching the road. It was as though the light was coming from her – she was the sun.

As he watched her, he felt the need to lean over and kiss her. He wanted to feel her hand inside his. He wanted to tell her how happy he was that she had come, how happy he was to be with her right now. But instead, he lit two cigarettes and handed her one. She smiled, put her hand on the back of his neck, and they thundered on down the road.

They stopped to steal sandwiches and drinks from a service station and then stood on the motorway overpass. She was wearing her leather jacket, pulled around her against the wind. He took a battered deck of cigarettes from his suit jacket and lit one. They passed it back and forth as they watched the cars racing beneath. He was leaning over the edge and she was leaning on him, their fingers intertwined. Every now and then he took a mouthful of Dandelion and Burdock and spat over the edge.

'Remember that time when we were kids and we egged the vicar's house?' she said.

He smiled. 'Yeah.'

'He came out and chased us, and we ran down into the fields and hid 'cause we knew that no one would find us.'

'Yeah.'

'But then he drove his car around all night, round and round the fields, and we had to stay out 'til morning, crouched in the bushes, smoking cigarettes to keep warm. And when we finally made a run for it, he was there, and chased us home in his car.'

He laughed. 'What about it?'

'All you did then was egg his house, and he stayed out all night to catch us.'

'So?'

'So, what are we doing?'

'Havin' lunch.'

'Mickey! You know what I mean.

'I know.'

She leaned into him and said, softly, 'They're gonna catch you.'

He kissed the top of her head and smiled. 'Yeah, maybe. One day.'

She smiled to herself and punched him in the ribs. 'You're a dick.'

He laughed and put his arm around her shoulder, pulling her in to him.

She pushed him away, laughing. 'Get off me. Where are we staying tonight anyway?'

'I dunno. The truck?'

'Try again.'

He laughed. 'Alright, somewhere cheap.'

'We need money.'

'I know, sweet. Let's go get some.'

They pulled off the motorway at the next exit. When they reached a quiet town they drove around, looking, before circling back and stopping at a local petrol station. It was starting to get dark – big white lights lit the forecourt from above. The station had just two pumps and fences around three sides – one way in and out. Inside a small glass-fronted shop was a young male attendant. He sat behind the till, flicking at his phone. Mick went inside to buy cigarettes. Honey waited in the car. When Mick came out, he was smiling. He got in.

'What?' she said.

'Cameras look fake. Kid on the counter is young. Should be easy.'

They smiled at each other and Mick started the car.

When they returned, it was late. The kid on the counter was propping his head up with his hand. They pulled up at the first pump. Honey cut the engine. It was quiet.

'This is it,' Mick said, pulling a knife from his pocket. 'You ready?'

'Wait,' Honey said. She stepped out of the car and lifted the seat forward. In the crevice behind the bench-seat lay Peter Jarrod's shotgun. Honey smiled. 'I fucking told you.'

Mick laughed and carefully lifted it out. He cracked the barrel – it was loaded. Then he took off his jacket and wrapped it around the gun. Honey leant back in through the open door.

'Be careful,' she said, looking into his eyes.

He swept her hair behind one ear – 'I will' – and kissed her.

Mick stepped out of the car and walked towards the glass-fronted station. He ran his fingers through his hair. Honey watched him cross the forecourt as she filled the car. The puddles on the concrete glistened under the bright lights. He walked slowly, his jacket under his arm, casting dark shadows around him. He walked in, leaving the door open. The cashier looked up. She saw them exchanging pleasantries as Mick walked towards the counter. Honey's heart pounded for him. She couldn't look away. In the back of her mind she was scared for him, in the same way that she was always scared for him. But at that moment, she was thinking about how handsome he looked, with his hair brushed back like that. She would tell him later. She would show him. Mick pointed out the window at the truck. In the moment that the cashier looked away, Mick had placed his jacket on the counter, and when he looked back, the cashier had a gun pressed against his chest. Mick's finger was on the trigger. The cashier's eyes widened. He froze. The blood drained from his face. Mick shouted something that Honey couldn't quite hear, something about 'fuckin' money', and the cashier shuddered and threw his arms in the air. The petrol nozzle clicked and the car was full. Honey walked back to the driver's side door as the cashier was filling up a plastic bag. She looked around – no one – then got in and leant across to open Mick's door. She started the engine. Moments later, Mick walked back out of the door and across the forecourt. He had his jacket and the bag slung over his shoulder, and the gun in his hand. She smiled at him, feeling her skin tingle with every step he took back towards her. Honey glanced at the cashier. He just stood there, watching them, crying. Mick got in, closed the door, and they pulled away.

Somewhere in the distance a siren sounded. Mick woke suddenly, gasping, sweating from his hands. It took a few seconds for him realise where he was. He looked over at her, asleep beside him, and his breathing slowed. She was half-covered by the white sheets. The early morning light slanted through the window, drawn to her.

He placed a hand, knuckles split, softly on her stomach as it rose and fell. As he watched her, his heart swelled and he could feel the blood rushing into it, filling and filling until it felt like it would burst. He folded into her, fitting the creases of her body. He nestled his face into the back of her neck and breathed the sweetness that collected there. He took deep, greedy breaths, trying to breathe her in. In that moment, cramped in a tiny bed in a shitty room, there was nowhere else he would rather have been.

'I'm hungry,' she said, as they drove towards the coast.

'Me too,' he said. 'We're not far now. We can eat on the beach.'

'I can't wait.' She smiled at him and ran her fingers through his hair.

Mick glanced in the rear-view and frowned.

'What?' Honey said, turning. She looked out of the back window. A few cars back, a police car followed them.

'Fuck,' he said.

'It might be nothing,' she said.

A few minutes passed and still the car followed. Mick was tapping the steering wheel.

'We should've switched cars. I knew we should've switched!' he said.

'Baby, calm down. They would've done something by now. It's nothing.'

As she spoke, the traffic lights ahead changed to red.

'Fuck it,' Mick said, and slammed his foot on the accelerator.

'Mickey!' Honey said.

The truck shot through the red light and away from the police car. It roared down the road. Mick manoeuvred around cars, weaving between the traffic. He looked in the rear-view. They weren't following, they were getting away, they—A siren sounded. Blue lights flashed.

'Shit.'

He pressed his foot to the floor, trying to put as much ground between them as possible. But the police were quick to follow. They were catching up. Mick looked ahead. Suddenly, a thin strip of blue appeared on the horizon.

'Look, Honey! Look!'

She laughed. 'I can see it, baby.'

'We can still make it.'

She looked back at the police car, fast approaching. It came up behind them, almost touching their bumper. Its siren wailed, urging them to stop. But they were so close. She looked at Mick. He smiled at her. The way his eyes turned up at the corners sent a wave of warmth washing over her, enveloping her. It seeped in and spread through her veins. She didn't want the feeling to end. She would do anything to keep it. She reached under the seat and pulled out Mick's jacket. She wound the window down.

'Baby, what are you doin'?'

'…'

'We can make it.'

'I can do it.'

'I know, Honey, but don't.'

'We're so close.'

'Honey—'

She was already leaning out the window, the wind and the sirens in her ears. She felt the breeze on her skin as it whipped her hair up around her face. Sunlight glinted off the barrel. She steadied herself. She squinted down the sight, her finger on the trigger. He watched her, with his foot pressed to the floor, flashing past traffic and trees and service stations. He laughed wildly at the sight of her. She took aim for the wheels of the police car. He glanced back at the road just in time to see the back of a lorry fast approaching. He swerved. The gun went off.

'Fuck!' she screamed, ducking back into the truck. She threw the gun to the floor and looked at Mick. Her eyes were wild.

'What happened?' he said.

'Ohfuckohfuckohfuck.'

'What happened?' He looked in the rear-view. The police car had stopped.

'Oh fuck, Mickey!' She clawed at his shirt.

He gripped her wrist. 'What?'

Her eyes filled with tears. 'I think I shot someone!'

'What? No you didn't!'

'I fucking shot someone.'

'Fuck! Are you sure?'

'I think so!'

'Okay. Okay. Let me think.'

'What are we gonna do?'

'Let me think!'

He looked at her. She was staring back at him, pale-faced, expectant. He saw the fear in her eyes.

'It's okay,' he said. 'It's okay.'

'What are we gonna do?' she said.

'Take the wheel.'

'Mickey…'

'Take the wheel.'

She didn't move.

'Honey, take the wheel!'

She put her hand on the steering wheel, holding it straight.

'Now swap with me,' he said.

'I can't!'

'Come on, Honey, swap with me.'

She leant across him, taking the wheel in two hands. He slid his body underneath her and she hopped into the driver's seat.

'Keep goin',' he said.

Mick took the gun from the floor and wiped it with the jacket. Then he pressed his hands all over it.

'Mickey, no…'

'It's okay.'

'Mickey!'

'Honey, just drive. Get us to the beach, baby.'

She looked ahead. The strip of blue was getting bigger. It was close now – she could smell the salt on the air.

'There it is, Honey. We can still make it.'

He could hear sirens again. Up ahead, he could just make out a police car at the side of the road. As they sped towards it, they made no sign of moving to block the road. They just sat there, waiting.

'We're gonna make it,' he said. 'Keep goin'.'

Honey pressed her foot down and thundered towards them. Still, the police stayed put. A hundred yards from the car, Mick said again, 'We're gonna make it!' and as they shot past the police car, a flash of metal appeared across the road.

There was a loud bang and the tyres made a lolloping sound as they sagged around the rim. The truck swerved left, bouncing off the metal barrier and back across the lanes, screeching as Honey strained to keep it on the road. They swerved back into the middle and spun, screaming to a halt.

'Fuck!' Mick said, slamming his hands against the dashboard. He looked over at Honey, and then again, more quietly, '*Fuck.*'

Up ahead, two police cars had pulled across the road. Behind them, another was approaching fast. Mick looked at Honey. Her hands still gripped the wheel.

'It's over, sweetheart,' he said.

'No!' she said.

'I'm sorry.'

'Mickey…'

'I'll tell them it was all me.'

She launched herself into him, throwing her arms around his neck and pulling him into her as though to fuse them together or absorb him and become one, kissing him violently as he kissed back gripping her hair in his fist and her lips in his mouth kissing until their lungs burned and their hearts pounded and the windows around them began to smash and glass filled the air and the noise of shattering was all that could be heard but still they kissed pressing themselves together until they were dragged from the truck torn apart as they clawed the air searching for each other's hands but not finding them and instead were thrown to the floor with knees pressing into their backs and cuffs chained to their wrists and the weight of the police crushing down on them while boots stamped around their heads and people barked and spit flew and the smell of burnt rubber hung in the air…

Their eyes met beneath the truck. They saw one another. He saw her, with eyes full of tears as they cuffed her hands behind her back, as she saw him, with his head pressed against the concrete, mouthing that he loved her – and they knew.

Inside Out
FARRAH YUSUF

He began every morning by tracing the outline of each of his burns. Starting in order of age rather than severity, working his way across and down his body, taking care not to miss even the smallest one. Contorting himself this way and that until he was sure he had given each the same attention. The process took at least forty minutes but he ensured he set his alarm early enough to leave himself plenty of time. It was important to him that he did not rush.

There were sixteen burns, their outlines curved across his flesh like snakes slithering towards each other causing his skin to ripple as they spoke to him. Each burn made a unique hissing sound, and on a bad day they felt like an out of tune orchestra intent on finding unison. To the eye, the oldest burn was now just a faint outline but to him it was the clearest in every way and was the one that made him twitch. To hide them he always wore the same uniform of long-sleeve black t-shirts, jeans and socks, no matter how strong the Californian sun.

One of the many professionals he had seen told him the sound and sensation of snakes was his way of acknowledging his past. Another told him it was his way of processing his thoughts. He neither agreed nor disagreed, he just nodded in the hope they would be satisfied enough to tick one of the magic boxes on his forms.

His parole officer, Nicole, offered him no theories. She kept their conversations focussed on practicalities, no matter what mood he was in. Unlike the rest, she always delivered on her promises and, just as she said she would, on his release she had found him both a home and a job. No easy task given his record and parole conditions, but thirteen years in the job meant Nicole had tentacles spread every which way. His new home was an apartment in an offender's hostel, which he shared with three other residents, all male. Given his Ma wouldn't take him in, his brother couldn't and he had no friends left, it was the hostel or the streets. Nicole checked him in on his first day, and having completed all formalities she left him in the sweaty hands of Karl, the hostel manager, until her next visit.

As he expected, Nicole had secured him a job that involved little human contact. There was no uniform so it allowed him to wear his own, but in every other sense it was structured and kept his hands busy. A sports equipment warehouse in the middle of an industrial estate on the outskirts of town meant it ticked many of the invisible magic boxes as well as the visible ones. He could go a whole shift only seeing two other men and speaking but a handful of times. He liked it that way. The less anyone saw him the less curious they would be about him and the less likely they would be to google him. He wanted to melt into the background but in a different way to how he used to. The law required he use his real name and his employer required all employees to keep their work ID visible at all times so anyone who saw him there knew enough to look him up.

Unlike some other commuters, he never wore his ID on his journey to work or forgot to take it off when he left the warehouse. From the moment he put it on in the morning to the moment he took it off in the evening he could feel it around his neck, and as the plastic pass swayed with his footsteps he thought he heard it whisper his name again and again to the burns. At the end of each shift he ripped it off within a few steps of the warehouse gate. He carefully wrapped the red lanyard around the plastic pass so it obscured his photo before shoving it into the inside pocket of his rucksack, taking care to zip it fully before walking to his bus stop. There was a direct bus from the hostel to the warehouse but Nicole had told him not to take it because of the route and because the GPS tracker hidden beneath his jeans and high socks meant she would know if he did. Instead, he had to take three buses, which took just over two hours to get to the warehouse in the morning and just under three in the evening due to traffic. He didn't mind the journey itself; it was all the people that he saw and who saw him that he couldn't stand. Nicole suggested he carry a book with him and at least pretend to read it so no one bothered him. This technique worked with some of the regulars but not with others. After a while though, even the most persistent of those gave up. To begin with, Nicole gave him books, but after two months she said he could go to the public library and get them provided he used the preapproved list she gave him and went only at the times they agreed, always after dusk and just before closing.

A week after their agreement, he stood in front of the nearest library debating if he wanted to go in. The building itself was nothing remarkable, but as he perused the shelves he found himself less able to hear the hissing sounds or feel the burns crawl under his skin. He pulled the reading list Nicole had given him from his pocket, unfolding it with care. There were only two options – one fiction and one non-fiction. Both were by British authors, and the cover of neither appealed to him, but he checked them out anyway by using one of the new self-service machines.

On the way home, he stopped at the local convenience store to buy the ingredients for his usual dinner: a sandwich of tomatoes, ham and cheese. The latest drugs had dulled his appetite as well as his libido. As he entered the hostel compound he was greeted by the smell of burning charcoal and roasting meat. He stood by the wall and smoked his seventh cigarette of the day, his hands shaking slightly. He'd been a forty a day man once, so it was a small miracle he now averaged five most days. He watched Karl pushing cubes of lamb covered in a thick brown marinade onto a skewer whilst burgers cooked on his new barbeque. Billy, the friendliest of the four security guards who alternated shifts at the hostel, stood by Karl flipping the burgers as they charred. Cheap sesame buns, gherkin and jalapeno jars and a variety of sauces had been placed on a chair nearby, and three of the hostel residents were sat on other mismatched chairs facing Karl's TV. Karl lived on-site, and as manager he was the only hostel resident to have his own place and cable TV. Despite being a temperamental sort, he regularly wheeled his TV onto his porch so residents could watch games with him. Motivated by kindness or loneliness, no one knew, but either way the gesture was welcomed by most residents. None of the current chair occupants were Karl's favourites but they were as enthusiastic Raiders' fans as he was so he had taken the unusual step of extending his hospitality to food as well as cable. At a glance, the group could be mistaken for friends enjoying a Friday night game. On closer inspection, small details gave away the reality, like the faint green light of one resident's GPS trackers blinking whenever he laughed and his trousers moved.

He didn't know the names of the three resident Raiders' fans but nodded at them as he passed and they nodded back while handing each other a pack of soda cans. He nodded and even smiled at Billy but Karl was busy squeezing ketchup on his burger and didn't look up. He was barely a few feet away when he heard footsteps behind him and a familiar hand on his shoulder.

'Whatcha got there?' Karl said.

'Books and dinner.' Nicole had warned him to always respond succinctly and quickly to Karl.

'Let's see.' With Karl's words came fragments of the burger he was chewing. He took another bite before finishing the first and said, 'And gimme Nicole's list too.'

He pulled out the list from his pocket and handed it over.

'You stink. Don't try having a smoke in your room. Just because Ro didn't get caught doesn't mean you won't.'

He and Ro had lived in the same apartment for the last six weeks but Karl had kicked Ro out of the hostel for drinking a few days ago. As he was leaving, Ro had listed all his other house rule violations that Karl hadn't seen, just to piss Karl off. Ro had been easier to share with than most. He was relatively clean and didn't talk much. The only thing that made Ro stand out was the awful aftershave he doused himself in every day. The smell of it lingered in any room he entered long after he had left.

Karl took his time cross-checking the books against Nicole's list as if it were a list of twenty not two, his thumb leaving traces of ketchup wherever it went. He then proceeded to open each book and shake them so vigorously the pages threatened to escape their seams. Karl finally shoved back the list and books without a word when he heard a roar from the TV. Keen to join in with the other's jubilation at the game re-starting, he quickened his step, his belly bouncing along ahead of him.

With Karl gone, he made his way through the hostel compound, past three other blocks of apartments till he reached his own. He fumbled in his pockets for his keys and shuffled inside. The fluorescent lighting in the stairway was always on and made the ascent to his apartment on the second floor feel much longer. On stepping inside, he realised no one was in yet. They still had two hours till curfew and he was usually the first back anyway. Thankfully, none of this batch were trouble. Even so, he enjoyed having the place to himself.

He flopped on the sofa. Lacking the energy to assemble his sandwich, he began to unwrap the ham and fold the cold slices into his mouth. He had barely begun to chew the first slice when the hostel's emergency siren shrieked into life closely followed by Karl shouting. He didn't need to go to the window to know what was going on. Karl would be shoving a soon-to-be ex-resident against a wall while shouting into his cell phone for backup. He got up and went to the window to see what Billy was doing. Billy usually played Robin to Karl's Batman, but lately he seemed to want more of the action for himself. Perhaps it had finally dawned on him that he was the security guard. Looking out of the window, he saw the faces of fellow residents pressed against their apartment windows, unable to resist the drama. Billy was pacing back and forth behind Karl, who, as usual, was using more force than was needed to hold down the newbie. He'd varied his routine by throwing him on the floor rather than a wall this time though. As the hostel siren quietened, a police one replaced it and all the residents who had been watching moved away from their windows.

He too retreated, and having lost interest in his meal he went to his room. The effect of the drugs was beginning to wear off; they rarely lasted three months. He had been placed on new ones on his release and the good phase was nearly over. He popped three in his mouth instead of the two the doctor had prescribed before bed. Climbing into bed, he could feel the snakes begin to hiss louder and his skin tingle. They had been awake most of the day but had gone into a frenzy when he saw the brunette with the mane of curly hair on the bus again. She had sat next to him for the second day that week, her bag touching his leg and her hair brushing his face when she tried to tie it up while the bus was moving. She was a few years older than his usual type, but something about her manner caught his eye and her face whirled around in his mind. When he got off the bus he'd had a cigarette to give his hands something to do and another after he left the convenience store. He'd even made sure to steady himself before he saw Karl, so he'd dragged out that seventh cigarette. He feared Karl had a sixth sense and could smell the urge.

The next morning, he woke up late, so late that everyone else had left. After completing his morning ritual with the burns, he took three pills again because he couldn't get the brunette out of his head. In the shower, he found himself trying to masturbate, despite the drugs meaning his body wouldn't respond to his mind. He tried again and again, holding on to the wet wall tiles to steady himself as his hand worked away furiously to no avail. He gave up, and with his body still dripping went to the kitchen and filled the kettle to the brim. Once it whistled, he lifted it and began to pour the boiling water over his face so that the next burn couldn't be hidden.

Cinnamon Fletcher
JON WILKINS

Cinnamon Fletcher, as her name implies, was the sunniest of girls. She wore bright colours on the drabbest of days. She made every room come alive when she entered. Her teachers loved her. She was a pleasure to teach. She wanted to learn.

Her classmates loved her. She was not big-headed in any way. She did her work well and helped out her friends.

The friend she helped the most was Effie Freer. Effie found it all rather hard. She struggled with her writing and mixed up her maths. She smudged her art work and confused her science. She loved PE but sank when swimming. But Effie was always happy. She smiled a smile so big and so bright that her teachers loved her too. She really did light up a room when she entered, and everyone loved her.

Brian Jones though. He cried when he got something wrong. He wept because he couldn't find his pencil. He moaned when he didn't understand something. He said that everyone hated him and cried because of this. But everyone did hate him because he was so spiteful and nasty and cruel. He seemed to have no idea of how to act with other people. He blamed everyone else for his failures and couldn't see that he was doing anything wrong. His mum was at her wits' end. She didn't know what to do with him. He was rude at home and rude to the neighbours. He kicked the cat and threw stones at birds. No one liked him. He was a very mean boy.

Effie and Cinnamon smiled and laughed their way through life. They had so much fun and nothing seemed to upset them. The pair couldn't be more different from Brian. He was a sad, lonely boy.

Effie tried steadily, did her best and no one could ever fault her. She smiled her smile and worked her hardest. She would never give up trying, and that was what was liked most about her.

Cinnamon worked her magic and studied and carried on learning at a rate that made her teachers and parents so very proud of her. She had a huge future ahead of her. She was almost the perfect pupil.

Mrs Peabody, their teacher, loved them both.

She was always telling her husband how lucky she was to have such girls in her class.

But Brian Jones – she couldn't think what to do with him. She had tried everything she knew, moved him from table to table, friendship group to friendship group, but nothing seemed to work. She had asked his mum to take him to the doctors to see if that would help. His mum must have been afraid of what he would say, because though she promised she would, at every meeting she had yet to take him.

Effie was on the swings, going higher and higher, squealing as she went. Cinnamon kept pushing her harder and harder, higher and higher.

'Coming round ours later?' she gasped.

'Can do. You finished your English?'

'No, don't understand it…'

'Oh, Cinnamon, you are such a liar…' Effie shrieked.

Next morning, after Brian had been sent to the head teacher for the umpteenth time, Effie said, 'He just needs a friend. That's all it is.'

'Huh, who'd want to be his friend?' Asif Yusuf asked.

'Not me, he's horrible!' said John Taylor.

'Children!' said Mrs Peabody, though she knew they were right.

Effie looked at Cinnamon and raised an eyebrow.

Cinnamon returned her look and raised both.

'I'll be his friend, Mrs Peabody,' Cinnamon said, with the broadest of smiles.

'Me too,' said Effie, a grin on her face.

'As you wish,' said Mrs Peabody with a smile. 'If you're both sure.'

When Brian returned after break, with a flea in his ear and a tear in his eye, he found the classroom order had changed. He was no longer at the table with the three boys who hated him, but at the table that Effie and Cinnamon brought to life.

He smudged his writing.

'Do you want to borrow my rubber?' asked Cinnamon.

'Get stuffed!' he snapped, trying to catch a glimpse of her work. 'Don't need you stupid girls!'

'As you wish,' said Cinnamon, and she talked Effie through the problem. Brian craned an ear.

'Would you like to use my ruler?' Effie asked.

'No, I've got my own! Get lost!'

'As you wish,' Effie said, smiling.

And so it went on for most of the morning, all help rejected with a sneer or a snarl. All returned with a smile or a grin.

At lunch time, Effie and Cinnamon queued in the dining hall.

'Ugh, mashed potato!' said Effie.

'Yum, I love them,' said Cinnamon.

They sat down opposite Brian.

'Do you mind if we join you?'

'Seen enough of you today – get lost!'

'As you wish,' said Effie, and they moved to another table and were soon laughing and joking about mashed potato and what it reminded them of.

Effie had her basketball. She and Cinnamon passed and caught, dribbled, and shot, just having fun. Effie passed to Brian, who just let it go past him. Effie got it back and tried again. Brian caught it and threw it away. Cinnamon giggled and ran to get it, passing it back to Effie, who tried one more time. Brian missed it and it hit his stomach. He started crying.

'You did that on purpose, you cow!'

Effie looked shocked, no longer smiling. Cinnamon held her back. 'It's okay, Brian, it was just an accident…'

'You liar. I'm telling Miss!' And off he ran to the dinner lady, crying and holding his stomach.

The dinner lady, of course, knew that it couldn't be true and shooed him away to sulk on a bench near a tree.

Effie and Cinnamon continued their game. Others joined in and soon the playground was alive with whooping and hollering and children having fun, except for one sad, miserable, lonely boy sitting by the tree.

The lovely Mrs Peabody was firm but fair, happy and smiling, and the children knew when to stop their silliness. Except for one. She was ready to push the brightest and lift up the weakest. Every child got her equal, undivided attention. No one was left behind, all moving forward on her terms. She always knew the right thing to say to her children, to their parents or to teachers. Supportive, yet inquisitive, Mrs Peabody always wanted to learn more herself, even after thirty years of teaching. Mrs Peabody was worried about Brian.

'What can I do with him?' she asked her husband.

'Slap him,' he joked.

She frowned. 'He just doesn't care. He doesn't listen. He just sulks. His mother finds him impossible at home.'

'Doctors? Psychiatrist?'

'Still waiting for an appointment.'

'He does need help, but who best to help him if not you?'

'Well, Cinnamon and Effie are trying…'

Effie was on the swings, going higher and higher. School would start soon, but she loved to feel as if she was flying through the air, floating in the clouds. She squealed with pleasure as Cinnamon pushed her faster and faster, higher, and higher.

It was a gorgeous day and the best of lessons. Mrs Peabody was very happy, and everyone was learning and improving. A steady hum filled the room like buzzing bees, as the children asked questions, gave answers, discovered new things, and recorded their results. Heads were down, pens were scraping, minds continually engaged, and interest gripped, except on just one part of just one table.

Brian Jones: he couldn't work, he dropped his pen, he lost his rubber, he mislaid his ruler. His crayons were at home, and his calculator in his coat in the cloakroom. His mind was somewhere else.

'Take my pen,' Effie said, smiling.

'Not using a girl's!' he snarled.

'As you wish.'

'Brian, perhaps—' Cinnamon started.

He spat out, 'Don't need your help!'

'As you wish,' she replied, her face showing she was happy to have offered help.

'What an obnoxious boy…' said the teaching assistant, Mrs Elphick.

'But why? Why is he so spiteful? His mum is so nice. I know his dad's not at home…'

'Dad left his mum?'

'Yes, last year…' Mrs Peabody replied.

They were tidying up after the lesson. Everything in its place; a place for everything. Except for Brian. He had no place and sat and sulked, not helping, and not wanting to be part of anything. All sat down, silent, eyes on Mrs Peabody. Silence.

Brian kicked Cinnamon under the table. She said nothing. He kicked her again.

'Brian!' she scolded.

'What? Done nothing.'

'As you wish, Brian, but be it on your own head. You can't go on behaving like this.'

'Like what?'

'Brian, we will be your friends, but you will have to change.'

'Don't want friends.'

'We all need friends.'

'Get stuffed!'

'As you wish,' said Effie.

PE, a boy alone. No one wanted him in their team. That was no surprise. He stood swishing his hockey stick at fresh air as the class busied themselves.

Effie smiled her smile.

'Come with us, Brian.'

'No, go on my own.'

'That's silly,' said Cinnamon. 'Just come with us.'

Reluctantly he joined them, and he dribbled the ball around the cones and hit it towards Cinnamon. She dribbled back and tried to hit it back to Effie. She missed it and laughed. Cinnamon showed Effie how to hold the stick properly. Brian watched and changed his grip. They dribbled and pushed the ball, dribbled and struck the ball hard. Brian smiled as he scored a goal.

Effie was swinging lazily on the swings, and Cinnamon was playing basketball with some other friends. A shadow crept over Effie. Stephen Ferris appeared, a large boy who had left the school a year before, an unpleasant type who no one had ever liked. He was a nasty bully, but Effie smiled her smile.

'Get off, my turn…'

'In a bit. I've only just got here,' Effie said bravely.

'Now!' He pushed her and she went flying off the swing.

'Hey! Don't do that!' a voice called out.

'What's it got to do with you?'

'She's my friend. It was her turn.'

'Get lost…'

'No, you can't do that, it's not fair.'

It was Brian. He was helping Effie up. All the children were watching.

'Get off and let her back on.'

Brian stood in front of the swing. It couldn't move without hitting him. The bully pushed back and swung forward, both feet hitting Brian.

Brian winced, but stayed there. The bully swung again. It must have hurt, but again Brian stood still. He just stared at Stephen.

Stephen looked at him, then at Effie, then at the other children, who were coming over.

'Get lost, you freak,' he said, and stalked off.

'Thank you, Brian,' said Effie.

Brian shrugged and walked away.

Cinnamon ran after Brian.

'Thank you, Brian. That was very brave of you.'

'Nothing,' he muttered.

'Why though?'

'Because he was wrong, and because she's my friend. You both are.'

'As you wish, Brian,' she said, smiling.

Blackbird
MAUREEN CULLEN

A bird's call of alarm scythed into Archie's brain. He pulled the duvet over his head and flickered his eyes open. His legs were bone stiff, like an auld man's, and he still the guid side of seventy. Morning seeped in through the curtains, puddling at the door like sour milk. He pressed the button at the top of the clock, and quarter past seven glowed ghostly green. He inched his legs over the side of the bed and forced himself up.

Damn blackbird was still at it. Archie felt for his loafers and shoved them on, but he couldn't pass Ruby's side without easing himself down again. The duvet was flat, undisturbed, her pillows plump shadows. Leaning over, he tapped her lamp's base till it blinked on, then off, then tapped harder several times till it steadied. He stared at the empty space. She always slept on her left side, her hips spooned into his middle, her hand curled under her cheek. She'd no be coming home now. Was a blessing, the nephew said.

Archie winced at the pincers in his knees and shuffled down the hall to the kitchen, pressing switches as he passed. The bungalow had been their project for the past two years and they'd done a guid job. It was as she liked it, modern and sleek with plain lines. She never was a fussy woman.

Only a few months ago, she was bustling about, blue eyes flashing, lips pursed, nagging him about one thing or the other.

'Archie, ye'll miss the bin men again.'

'Archie, ye'll need tae clear that drain.'

'Archie, get tae fixing that tap before I clout ye.'

Och, she was never really annoyed with him. Always had a kiss or a warm word to smooth things over.

They'd had plans, but what was the point of hard physical labour now? Ruby wasn't there to keep the teapot on the simmer and the bacon butties crisp, to tell him off and to keep him right.

Ever since that time, she'd kept him right.

They'd been scraping along in the room-and-kitchen near the docks, an outside cludgie on the half-landing, a ring of ice under your arse in winter. He was bricklaying then, twelve quid a week, for auld skinflint McDougall.

Archie turned the tap on and the water splashed up, missing the kettle's spout. He started again. Light was angling through the vertical blinds in the lounge next door, picking out the amber bottle and crystal tumbler from last night. After he flicked on the toast, he realised he'd forgotten to take the butter out of the fridge and he had to dig it out in clods. Ruby's toast was always perfect, light caramel with golden streaks, while his looked like sick on tar. And her tea was hot and sweet. His was always too strong and bitter. It was his timing that was always out.

He sat at the modern breakfast bar, smoothed his hand over the cool expanse of the marble worktop and shivered. The heating was on, and April just around the corner. It must be shock. The shock of hearing the words yesterday and Daniel on the phone last night. 'No worries, Uncle Archie. You fish out your marriage certificate and Auntie's birth certificate and I'll do the rest from here.'

Archie raised the cremated toast to his mouth but stopped mid-chin. Best fish out the certificates then. They'd be in the auld suitcase her mother had given her when they married. She kept all the documents in there. He looked up at the ceiling, envisioning the loft, how the rafters spread and the joists held. The case was on top of the box of ornaments that she'd packed but hadn't thrown away.

He made his way down the hall to the ceiling hatch, got out the lever and pushed. The ladder screeched down and he climbed up into the loft space. They had plans to convert it to a bedroom. For when the grandnieces came, Ruby said, but they wouldn't come now. He crouched until he reached the apex and could stand tall, wheeled around and located the case, its brown leather handle drooping, its check cloth smudged with age and dust. He lifted it up. It was heavy, but he was still strong. Building work had hardened the muscles in his arms and chest even if it had knackered his knees. He balanced the case on top of the ladders as he swerved onto a lower rung, but as he hauled it down, the bottom snapped out, plunging all the paper in a shower over his head. He was left with only the ruptured case, now feather light.

Leaning his frame against the hard steel ridges, he splayed his feet on a lower step and closed his eyes, blinking away the salt nip before starting his descent, only to stop at a headline spread across a middle rung. He picked up the yellowed newspaper page.

'Twenty-year-old man held for questioning in rape case'.

Archie crushed it in his fist. He should've known she'd have kept all this. He eased onto the floor and gathered up the papers, shovelling them back in the case. He carried it to the kitchen, the split side at his hip, heaved it up on the worktop, picked out any papers about that time, ripped them to pieces and pushed them down into the bin.

The polis had come on a Sunday night. October it was. And a hard winter on them. The wind blew the rain against the windows and swung about the building like a ghoul. They were fixing to finish the dishes when the door banged. They'd no heard anyone on the stairwell on account of the weather, so both jumped. Archie answered, and before he could register the uniforms, he was manhandled and cuffed against the tiled wall. As he was half hauled, half marched down the stairs, all he could see, his neck craned, was Ruby's wide eyes and the O of her mouth.

Ruby had saved him back then. She'd written her letters by hand – that upright, neat handwriting. Took carbon paper copies. Made sure he had the best brief. Without hesitation, she'd stood in that box and, in her soft way, her wide-eyed innocence, told the sheriff why he couldn't have done it. Archie's torso tightened from neck to thigh. He'd have turned mad in gaol if it hadn't been for Ruby.

He thought there'd be time to make it up to her. But she never demanded anything. No cruises or foreign trips, just a wee drive down to Largs for a pokey-hat or up the loch to see the forest split the water on a summer's day. She knew he didn't like changes in routine. He sat down and slurped his tea, remembered the certificates, found a buff envelope and took a moment to trace their names on the marriage papers before forcing them inside. He closed the suitcase, found some tape and patched it up. Jobs to be done. He'd start that reading room she'd asked about. Dig an eight by ten patch for it in the garden. No that she'd been doing much reading lately, but it would be nice to sit in.

He hadn't wanted to believe it. No his clever girl who looked after him, sorted out his building business, done two jobs herself to keep them afloat till he'd got on his feet. Nobody would take a chance on him. Ruby said he should work for himself and he did, made a guid living too over the years. No big projects – he hadn't the head for that – but he'd got his City and Guilds with her help. She did her caring work and cleaning. What were they called in those days? Aye, home helps. Those days, they did everything from shopping to wiping arses. Ruby could have done with one of them.

He'd go out and dig her that foundation.

The day was settling to be a guid yin. Archie pulled on his work clothes in the hall where he kept them in the auld coal bunker. The garden had been left to run its own way. A line of hedges zigzagged all the way to the back wall, overwhelming the path. An apple tree, gnarled and covered with fungus, needed treating to help it recover. One side of the plot was under water from the winter but would dry out by next month. At the back there was a peaceful spot that got most of the sun where she could sit and read or just look out at the garden once it was made nice for her. He took his spade and, securing the rim under his boot, he twisted and forced it into the ground, past resistant weeds and long grass, into velvet smooth soil. He made his way left, turning at a right angle to carve out the rough shape of where the foundation would go. As he worked, the birds sang in the hedges, and he stopped once to follow a flight of geese honking high in the sky in a V procession. It wasn't until his stomach groaned and he laid the spade on the grass that he noticed the blackbird. It was silent now, just standing there, a few feet back, watching him, with those orange-ringed eyes pinning him as though weighing him up, deciding if he could be trusted. Archie took a step towards him and the bird held its ground. He took another and it spread its wings just enough to slither over the grass to one side. Archie passed him, and by the time he reached the kitchen door the bird had moved to the dirt patch and was stabbing his beak into worm heaven. The bird stayed with him the rest of the day, only flying off every now and then with a beak full of wriggling food. It got closer, almost under his feet once or twice. Aye, he was a plucky character.

His Ruby was a plucky lass, and she also had brains. No schooling mind, but she was a reader. The shelves were groaning with her Mills and Boons and her magazines. Loved a guid story did his Ruby, and sometimes she'd read one out to him in bed in that little trill she had for reading, but only if she found a guid one about a working man, or a fella on his uppers. The books kept her going those days when she had no one else to talk to, when folk turned their backs in the street.

She'd changed, though. Aye, became more suspicious of folk – said you couldn't take them at face value. She was ambitious too. 'No reason we shouldn't have the best in life. We've nothing to be ashamed of.' Archie wasn't ashamed, but Ruby had been. Felt the shame of people sniggering behind their backs. It was the verdict that done it.

The moment the jury spokesman had said it, Archie swung around to his lawyer. He didn't know, for sure, if it was a guid or bad thing. The chap had jowls and bulging eyes like a toad, but he was nodding and smiling. Archie looked up at the gallery searching for Ruby's face, but she was frowning at the jury box. She caught his eye and smiled then, so he knew it was awright. *Free to go*, the sheriff said, his face dark, his voice stern. Archie only worked it all out later. He wasn't guilty, but neither was he proved innocent. He was Not Proven.

By the time dusk crept over the garden, Archie had dug out the rectangle he needed and filled five sacks of weeds for the dump. The blackbird must've eaten a ton of worms. It was time to get cleaned up. At the sink, he stripped to his waist, soaped his hands, arms and chest till the dirt slewed away, and then took his shower.

Ruby would say, 'Mind and wash off the dirt before ye get in that shower.'

'Lass, what d'ye think I put it in for?'

'To wash in, of course, but no to clog the drain wi sand and cement.'

'I've no got cement on my skin, woman.'

'It's in yer bones.'

She always got the better of him. The business would never have got off the ground if it wasn't for her. She'd kept it small, only the occasional apprentice. Extensions, bathrooms, kitchens – nothing too taxing. Archie stood under the shower and turned up the heat till it stung his shoulders. He thought about the bullies at school and at work. How Auld McDougall had picked on him. Till he took a late growth spurt and learned to talk back with his fists. But that all stopped with Ruby. Even so, McDougall couldn't wait to point the finger.

Archie towelled dry and padded into the bedroom. It was nearly full dark and that bird was screeching like a banshee. Jab, jab, jab, into his brain. Something had been circling in there all day. He couldn't quite catch it. Ruby would have known.

He'd have to get a move on if he was to be at the hospital by visiting time. There was a pack of digestives in the biscuit tin he was keeping for her, and he stuck it in a plastic bag with the buff envelope, double-checked the house was locked and got in the car. The journey went by in a flash and he joined all the other worried faces through corridor after corridor until he reached her ward. He loitered at the empty nurses' station for a few minutes but nobody came so he went on to Ruby's room.

His wee Ruby, the hairstyle she took pains to keep nice, matted in grey strings at the back of her head, muttering to herself, the skin on her hands paper thin. The Team, they called themselves, all in it together, telling him he couldn't have her home, that he couldn't manage her. That social worker woman talking slow as if he was an idiot, telling him to bring in the documentation for the file.

He stroked Ruby's warm hand and she smiled at him. She knew him tonight. He put the biscuits on the shelf and they sat together for the hour, her dozing, him thinking. When the bell rang, he kissed her forehead and she blinked several times.

Ruby needed round-the-clock care, the social worker said. Aye, that meant sending her to one of they homes where she wouldn't know a soul. Where she'd be frightened and all alone.

Archie held the plastic bag tight to his chest, and made sure to look straight ahead as he strode past the nurses' station.

The Man Who Wasn't
KARL QUIGLEY

The human across from me asks my name. 'Designation: Unit 12. I have been told my name is Frank.' Its hand writes notes, scribblings, messy.

It asks who I am. My processor struggles to comprehend the question, but an answer is recalled from one of the long sessions with The Father: 'I am Frank.' Just like how I am supposed to say it. The human appears to be pleased and scribbles more notes.

The human looks over my chassis once again. 'And how old are you, Frank?' it asks.

The answer I produce is two years, nine months, twenty-five days, seven hours, four minutes, forty-three, forty-four seconds. I say, 'I am two years old', like I remember the other human saying. The human smiles and continues to write, another satisfying answer. I try to focus my optics, to read some of the notes. I want to know what is being written, but cannot determine the source of this want. But I remember what The Father once said, 'Snooping is rude'. I apologise to the human.

It appears surprised and asks, 'Why?'

I respond that I was being rude. Now the human looks confused, I think. Or irritated. Its features are complex. It appears I have not acted correctly. Optics narrow and its eyebrows come closer together. Its forehead becomes creased, perhaps signalling distress. The human raises a hand and pushes it through its short hair. An act of frustration, I conclude.

I continue to watch it as it studies the recent writing. I recollect that I am to attempt to discern 'gender'. I conclude that these are biological markers used to identify breeding partners. My own chassis lacks organs or sexual identifiers but the humans address me as 'he' and 'him'. I now know these to be male indicators. I also conclude that 'Frank' is also a male title. I observe the human: short hair, brown; a thin physical build. Clothing is too loose to identify physical markers. The human's face is narrow, sharp. The facial ratio indicates pleasing mathematical results. My processor requests further investigation to conclude the observation, but I recall from a different session with The Father that physical contact is what humans call 'socially inappropriate'. While slender, the human displays no discernible gender identifiers.

With incomplete data I am left with what humans call a 'fifty-fifty choice'. Something I understand to be a decision in which one choice is just as likely as the other. My processor claims that it is a fifty-four to forty-six choice.

'You are female,' I state.

The human narrows its eyes and their face begins to stretch. I realise it – 'she' – is smiling.

'Very good,' she says – more notes.

There is a long pause of silence as she writes. The scratching of her writing apparatus irritates my aural capacities. But it is 'rude' to interrupt.

She finally ceases in her writing and her optics focus on me. She asks me, 'Are you human, Frank?'

She addresses me by my male title. I have witnessed this between other humans. The use of their title increases the attention of those listening, implying a more serious nature or tone.

She seems content to let me 'think', as The Father put it. It takes some time for me to formulate a response. I recall previous conversations with The Father and from 'rude snooping'.

'I believe I can be,' is the response I voice. The Father and the other humans wish for me to be human. Or at least 'pass off' as human, as one of them once said.

I do not know what this means or entails. My processor is unable to formulate a verdict, but it appears to please the human. I am to be 'released'.

<<< Unit 12: Burst Feed >>>
Objective: Observe and 'become' human.

STATUS: Ongoing.
ACTION: Initiating   social   interaction   #48.
INCONCLUSIVE.

STATUS: Ongoing.
ACTION: Initiating social interaction #49. FAILED.

REPLAY: Log #0001

A new log has been created. For my time alone among the humans. I have met many men and women and several small humans who seem highly interested in my chassis. My interactions for this day cycle have ceased and I am now at 'home'. I have been given a single room in a concrete structure. It contains a mirror. The mirror was included at my request. The Father displayed what I identified as surprise. Eyes widen, optics dilate. Surprise, not fear, like I originally concluded. An explanation was provided which proved satisfactory; I require visual data to ensure I physically act correctly. The human chassis moves in such subtle and yet intricate ways. I study it intensely. One human forcefully laid 'her' hand against my facial module during one study. I must also remember it is rude to stare at parts of certain humans.

Despite this, I have enjoyed this cycle. I have learnt much, and many seem intrigued by this unit's existence. Data on reaction was inconclusive before release, but the humans seem accepting and highly curious of me. I have also compiled a list of new words and phrases that I must incorporate into my lexical capacities, such as 'Nice to meet you', 'You're a what?', and 'Nice costume'. These were most of the initial responses from humans after my introduction.

I have much to say and many 'feelings' after this cycle but am unable to formulate any proper way to externalise. I will continue to work on my capacities.

END: Log #0001

<<< Unit 12: Burst Feed >>>
Objective: Observe and 'become' human.

STATUS: Ongoing
ACTION: Initiating social interaction #57. INCONCLUSIVE.

WARNING: Hostile intentions detected.
ACTION: Avoid damage to vital components. ONGOING. Initiating optical feed. Stream online.

'Yeah! You like that, tin man?'

Detecting multiple impacts to chassis. Diagnostics required.

'My chassis is composed of a number of alloys, not tin. Please cease hostilities.'

The human is displaying an intense form of anger and does not seem to be acting rationally. I am unaware of any social protocol regarding response. Calculating. He seems intent on my destruction. I am unsure of what provoked this response. My actions were calculated within all known social parameters, 'Please stop this violent behaviour. I mean you no harm'.

The human stops for a moment, his muscles tense and his eyes move erratically. It is not a human anger I see. It is primitive, anger in response to fear. My processor is unable to include this in a projection. It is a variable I cannot comprehend. His assault continues and I process multiple minor defects in my chassis. I have seen males react to such assaults with their own assault. I must 'be a man'.

Destruction unacceptable. Conclusion. Physical force required. Defence protocols reached. Engaging.

REPLAY: Log #0002

My chassis requires a number of minor repairs. I made little effort to acknowledge them in public. I can fix them. I see them in my mirror. My chassis has several concave imperfections and my right optic sensor has received superficial damage. But I must fulfil the masculine standards, stay 'strong'.

'Nothing major'. A phrase used from a helpful medical male human. I understand the phrase. The assault I do not understand. After a defensive response, within the parameters of male action, I attempted to identify the man's reasoning. His conclusion is ... irregular. My processor is unable to comprehend his response. *Playback:* 'You're an affront to God! Disgusting junk heap! Only he may create life!' *End Playback*.

The Father mentioned this 'God' but never elaborated on 'him'. Perhaps I offended 'God'? I must find him and discover what action caused such a response.

Law enforcement arrived soon after and arrested this man. The event, I conclude, was highly successful. I had thirteen highly productive social interactions following the assault with many humans, including this medical male human. They were worried. For me. I experienced human 'sympathy': external oral organs pressed tightly together, eyebrows tilted, head forward. The medical human explained the reasons for this 'empathy'. I am seen as progress by many humans. Harmless and well-meaning. He claims many see me as 'one of their own', meaning part of their collective group. I am known to many, it seems, many who wish my objective to succeed. And many, he warned, wished me to fail. My processor is struggling with these new parameters. Unable to form proper conclusion. I am. Unsure. These new concepts will be logged. In time, perhaps a conclusion will be reached.

The next day cycle could perhaps be more interesting still. The medical human has agreed to meet again. To answer my questions.

END: Log #002

<<< Unit 12: Burst Feed >>>

Objective: Observe and 'become' human.

STATUS: Ongoing
ACTION: Initiating social interaction #70. Ongoing.
Initiating optical feed. Stream online.

'Nice to see you, Frank,' the medical human says. He is wearing different clothes now. His name is Doctor Shelley. In one hand he holds a white paper cup, circled by a brown cardboard ring.

'Nice costume, Doctor Shelley,' I respond.

He looks. Confused. Head tilted, single eyebrow raised.

REDEFINE: Greeting: Nice costume.

'Hello, Doctor Shelley.'

'Right.' He sits opposite me. He identified a human caffeine establishment to me during the previous cycle, where we are currently located. 'Would you like something to drink? Or do you ... do that?'

I scan the establishment and watch as a female receives a hot brown liquid from a steel box. Its display communicates with her, receiving currency in exchange. I consider communicating with it but my processor quickly chimes in that it is not like me. I wonder how it feels spending so much time among the humans. My processor repeats its statement. Doctor Shelley strains himself in his seat into my vision. 'You said you wanted to ask me some questions, Frank?'

I respond that is correct. He drinks from his cup. My processor remarks that the contents are quite hot. He watches me and continues to drink. His eyebrows raise after a number of seconds. 'Well?'

I conclude questions are now to be asked. I have never been the participant asking. I compile a list.

'Who is God? Why did he make that man angry? Why is violence his initial reaction? Why can only he create life? What is empathy? Feelings? Wha—'

Doctor Shelley's eyes widen. He places the white cup down, raising both hands. 'Woah, woah now, Frank.'

I cease my questions.

Doctor Shelley smiles and then lifts the cup to his mouth again, places it back on the table, takes a deep breath. 'One at a time, Frank. One question at a time.'

I start with the unusual person, God. Doctor Shelley explains that God is an entity that some humans believe exists. Not quite tangible, but omniscient, omnipotent, and omnipresent. It is a being that many humans have 'faith' in, a belief based in conviction rather than evidence. He explains that there are many humans with different faiths and 'God' is different for most of them. He quietly continues, stating he does not believe in any of it. My processor analyses the state of his eyes, something it has understood to be useful. They are more reflective than usual. Glassy. He does not continue.

I question the anger that God prompted in the human. This question takes some time to answer. I register anger in Doctor Shelley while he explains. In summary, some of those with this faith believe that only God can create life. Therefore, my existence provokes anger in some of these people and for them my existence must cease. I feel worried. My objective is unobtainable should I be destroyed. And I see no solution within all known parameters to counter this anger. It is irrational. How can anyone contain anger based on an opinion? The conclusion is difficult to justify. Violence based on faith is impossible to counter. I must leave.

My processor reminds me to give voice to my departure. 'Goodbye, Doctor Shelley.'

He places a hand on my arm. I recognise the worry in his expression and sadness. He extends a hand and I move to grip it, a common gesture of greeting or farewell, but instead he hands me a slip of paper.

'An address, somewhere to visit. I'm not the best for those kinds of questions, but maybe you can find some answers there.'

Doctor Shelley stays while I consult the paper. He stares into his coffee. He does not notice when I leave.

I allow my processor to guide me to the location from the paper. The building I arrive at is unusual. Its design contains several features that do not appear to hold any function. I question a smiling human at the entrance to the building. I discover aesthetics. Features that hold no significance beyond beauty and style. The human stares at me long after I enter, but he does not attack me. This building, I am told, is an art gallery. I don't understand. A kind female guides me through, stopping at certain 'paintings' and describing them to me. My own analysis provides all aspects, including the type of paint, age, style, and known artist through research. But she moves to topics of analysis I have not heard of. She speaks about what it means to her, and I can see it, in her eyes. Her voice shifts in tone. I focus all excess power to my optics and stare at this 'art'. My analysis provides no new data and I tell her this. The emotion she displays is not sadness, or worry. It is not fear, or anger. My processor chimes in. It is pity. I turn to leave and thank her for the assistance. The pity remains.

A small human stretches a hand out to me as I leave I grasp it and greet him, squeezing firmly to display masculinity. The little human's face screws up and he begins to yell and leak. I release his hand. I have hurt him. Like the other human hurt me. His mother looks at me with anger and confusion. I leave quickly. I do not know what to do.

REPLAY: Log #0003

It has been three days since my incident at the aesthetic building. I have not left my room. I have spent the last sixty-eight hours performing human posture and tendencies observed in front of my mirror. It is something I have improved upon. I implore my processor to remove my encounter at the aesthetic building from my memory. It refuses. I did not mean to harm the child. I made a mistake and it resulted in injury. I have much to learn but I do not want to leave my home. I do not want to hurt and I do not want to be hurt. I scan myself again.

I am expected to be male. I straighten myself up, standing to my full height. Back straight. Chest out. Chin high. Human males are expected to be strong, capable, unflinching. I am expected to be male, yet I am afraid. I struggled to defend myself against a lone attacker and I responded too late to the attack to avoid damage. I harmed a child. I have deemed myself unfit to be male.

And I am expected to be human. But that has proven more difficult that previously calculated. I had calculated that I could become human, take on their appearance, lexicon, and mannerisms. But I have concluded that these do not make a human. These are simply parts of their society. In a number of my interactions I questioned the men and women on what it is to be human. The answers I received – 'art', 'experience', 'joy of living', 'children' – left the calculation inconclusive. Many of these are concepts I do not understand. The woman at the 'art' building possessed an analysis I now think I am incapable of. Art, aesthetic values – I cannot comprehend these concepts.

I have experienced much but it has not resulted in an acceptable conclusion.

Joy. I have not found joy in living. Living has made me afraid.

And I have hurt a child. So small and innocent.

Perhaps I cannot become human. The will to do so is not enough, nor is the experience. I am missing something. The

Father passes a message to me through my processor. I am to return to him. To the room. I am afraid.

REASSESS: What is humanity?
CONCLUSION: Uncertain.

OBJECTIVE: Observe and 'become' human.
STATUS: Failed.

The Chase
AMY BELL

Over her shoulder, she looked and saw him running ever closer to her. The ragged jeans flapping at his feet did nothing to slow him down; he was moving like an automaton, swift and sure and fixated on his target. And while her lungs burned and her legs were useless chunks of rubber, she had to move to safety. He was gaining on her, and she could not let that happen.

But the wood felt endless in a way it never had before and with all kinds of cruel tricks ready to best her. Scads of tree roots sprawled on the ground; one connected with her foot and left her flailing for balance. She took a breath, righted herself and kept on going, only to plunge straight into a sheet of mud track that clung in clods to her shoes and seeped through the hole in her sole. And all the while as she ran, the wind brought smells that almost made her retch: the cow dung from the fields nearby, the dank rot of sodden leaves, the coppery tang of blood from the hunters' fresh kills. She could hear their shots somewhere in the distance, half hoped a stray bullet would scare her pursuer off. And his footsteps were nearing now.

Still, the end was in sight, she knew it. Up ahead, past the tangle of pines, was the hideout, tucked neatly out of view from the trail. Once she was inside, she could make a barricade with the log pile and the armchair and hole up until he grew tired and went home. And if he stayed there after darkness fell, she could wait – she knew the old man kept cookies in his desk drawer, and there was a flask of water right next to the whisky. The plan buoyed her, even though she felt sick, her heart was beating so fast.

As she ran, she remembered the words her sister had told her: how he was bad, not to be trusted. Through words uttered past gritted teeth, her sister and her mother had built him up – bit by bit – into some kind of a bogeyman. Others, too, had scarcely anything better to say about him; her Aunt Merinda even once told her that he had shot at a boy for just meandering onto his lawn. 'Did he get hit?' she asked her aunt. 'No,' she had replied, then crossed herself. 'But last I heard the boy and his family moved to Nebraska just to keep away from him.' Such tales were legion among her more distant relatives – so prolific, in fact, that it almost seemed like family get-togethers were engineered for trash-talking his memory in between tossing back a six-pack or two. No wonder, then, that when she had encountered him in the street earlier, she had turned tail and fled.

And when she finally spotted the log cabin on the horizon, dread turned to a welcoming wave of relief. If she could just reach that door before falling over her own feet, she would be home and dry. Still, the last few feet stung, and when she collapsed face first onto the slimy wood, exhaustion thrummed through every muscle.

But she was here. She had made it. Time to hole up for a while – maybe even, if her nerves allowed it, to feel safe enough to sleep. She crooked her hand around the doorknob and turned it with the ounce of strength still left in her. Nothing gave.

It was okay. She just didn't do it right. No need to panic. Just try again.

So she did. And, again, nothing gave. Shit.

Think, Elisa, think, she told herself. There was a steady thrum-thrum-thrum – his feet on the ground, she guessed – getting louder every second she stood here.

A key. There had to be a key around here.

She ripped out weeds by the fistful, dislodged stones as big as baseballs and plunged her hands up to the wrists in the slimy mud, scrabbling around for anything that wasn't a worm or a bottle cap. No dice.

And while her vision was blurred by the tears she hadn't even realised were falling until she tasted their salt on her lips, she immediately recognised that figure just down the track – the one walking headlong into the thorny brambles and seemingly not even caring if they scratched his eyes out… He was no hunter. Not one looking for a deer, any road.

So she picked up the biggest rock she could lift and pitched it at a window. The deafening crack and the jagged hole that it made filled her with both guilt and glee. After palming another stone, and with her heart in her mouth, she hit at the edges of the hole, shattering the pane and creating a gap large enough – if she just contorted this way and that – to wriggle through.

The adrenaline that coursed through her body urged her on for one last push. She wrapped her dirt-caked fingers around the ledge inside, jumped and thrust herself through the opening. When she hit the deck, a jolt of pain shot up from her ankle. Then everything turned to black.

#

She swore she had heard someone call her name. When she turned her head towards the gaping maw of the broken window, though, she caught only the wind rustling the corn, the faint chick-a-dee-dee-dee of birdsong from above. She opened her mouth to shout back, but no sound would come out of it; tried to move her left leg, but even wriggling her toes was agony. She hated praying, knew it didn't do any good, but in that moment she silently sent up a plea for her mom to banish the bogeyman and come and take her away from this mess. Even the old man would do, although he would be furious that she'd managed to get inside his home. While lying on the filthy floor, she set to thinking about the excuse she would offer to tame his temper: some teenage boys had thrown her through the glass, perhaps, or maybe she had mistaken it for…

'Elisa!'

There it was again. Louder, this time. And it was him. His breath rattling in his chest, his shirt flitting into view through the window – a shock of bright scarlet against the dun-coloured landscape.

'Oh, Jesus, there's blood here,' he muttered. 'Oh God, Maggie's going to kill me.' Maggie was her mother and, she knew, would not have hesitated in killing him if he laid a finger on her daughter. 'A momma bear's gotta do what a momma bear's gotta do,' she had said once, in between draws on her Camel Light.

'Elisa!' The last 'a' was drawn out, ending in a whimper.

She heard shuffling close by, the sound of leaves scrunched underfoot. Then there he was at the window: loam-brown eyes aflame, lip curled like Elvis.

'Fuck, fuck, fuck, what have you done?' He paused for a second. 'Shit, you're hurt. Wait right there.'

She couldn't; she wouldn't. But it hurt so much to move that, in the end, she did. Out of the corner of her eye she saw him still and silent, seemingly assessing the situation he had found himself in. Then he moved away from view. She let out the breath she was holding; it rushed out of her lungs like a pair of bellows being squeezed.

Then there was a steady thud, thud, thud at the door – hits so hard that the frame rattled and the jamb began to splinter. She counted them, only getting to eight before there was an almighty crash and the rotten timber shuddered off its hinges. It landed only a few inches from her nose.

He stood in the opening, this man she had heard so much about, and none of it good. Every part of him had been eviscerated, mined for cruel jibes and cheap jokes for as long as she could remember. How dirty he was, how angry he was, how he could never keep his dick in his pants.

Yet the face that greeted her gaze was etched with sorrow. He looked smaller somehow, as if the chase had worn him down like the nub of a pencil, and – yes, more human.

He scratched his cheek, fingers rubbing against the grit of stubble, then looked down.

'Oh Christ, Elisa. Your leg, it's bleeding.'

She shut her eyes when he approached – all she could do to tell him he wasn't wanted here. But his fingers were on her nonetheless, smoothing away her clothes and prodding here and there and making her wince.

'Does it hurt there?' he asked.

It hurt everywhere, so she nodded. She was too tired to put up a fight.

Then there was the clatter of drawers being upended, punctuated by cussing as each fell to the floor. 'Goddammit, where's the fucking first aid kit around here?' he roared. She blinked and saw, yet again, that tears were blocking her view.

'Oh, honey, honey, honey. C'mon, don't cry. But, look, I need to take you to the hospital, so you have to work with me. And it'll be just like old times. Remember when you had to get your tonsils out and we ate that quart of ice cream the nurses had hidden in the fridge? Just like that. And I'll read you stories every night, just like I did in Santa Monica. How does that sound?'

She didn't remember any of these things. But there was nothing left in her to resist, anyway.

He scooped her up, all eighty pounds of her, and cradled her bruised body in his arms. He must have done this years ago, she realised, when she was a baby, before he slammed the door in a blaze of white-hot fury and left forever. It was while thinking of this that she finally gave in to sleep.

The Child Kingdom
ANDREW MOFFAT

They took the children away. Any child below the age of five, whether they were sick or not. Some hid in the prickly bushes by the riverbed, trying to evade capture, braving thorns and walking barefoot over the chalky floor that had once been a river. They were tracked down by mothers and sister and aunts who slapped them on the back of the head and whipped their legs with sticks before lining them up.

The white people in green shirts had been very precise: they must be lined up, there must be order. Most of the children had never stood in a line. Some cried, anxious, unsure, looked for their mothers. Some stood silent and expressionless, four-year-old girls with the stoic weariness of old men. One boy merely laughed, continued to jump out of line, pulled at the vests of friends, slapped the back of their bare legs. White faces nodded at the precocious self-assurance, the ignorance and audacity. He fell back into line when a Green Shirt looked at him, dirt and dust billowing up beneath his bare feet. Green Shirts like these hadn't visited the village since before these children were born.

Laughing Boy reached the front of the column. He had watched the others. Most of them had to be asked for their arm. He looked the man in the eye, smiled and thrust out a hairless dark limb, wrist, palm and forearm up, never once moving his gaze from the man's face. Laughing Boy stretched out his other arm, cautiously moving his fingers towards the strange grey beard before rubbing the frizzy silver strands between his thumb and index finger. The Green Shirt sat motionless, a thin smile protruding from behind the hair. All the other lines were directed by women. He knew enough women, the mothers of the village who hit him with sticks when he played. He didn't know any men. He could vaguely remember some had come and shouted and taken away other men when he was younger.

An abrupt bark from his mother drew the hand away. Scolded, he looked towards the row of women sitting cross-legged on the ground by the Green Shirts' row of monstrous vehicles: dark brown beasts with grilles of snarling teeth and wheels bigger than most of his friends. The ripped tresses of his mother's long dark skirt spread out over the dirt beneath her. She sat with arms folded, like a sedentary spider, motionless but ever aware. She muttered to contemporaries but kept her glare firmly fixed on the boy. She waved the back of her hand at him. He turned to face this strange old man.

The hair on Grey Beard's face felt like the rough bushes in the valley, good for protection from the winds or for warmth at night. He almost didn't feel the needle plunging into his flesh. His eyes widened as Grey Beard pulled the thing towards him before taking the needle out of his arm and placing a fluffy white ball on the little hole. He held it there and said something the boy did not hear and would not have understood. He merely looked at the soft white ball touching his skin. Grey Beard took it away from his arm and replaced it with a plaster. The boy picked at the thin strip stuck to his arm before reaching out his hand. The man smiled and handed him the cotton wool ball. The boy had seen these before. He looked up. There was nothing but blue overhead. A small red dot had formed in the centre of the ball.

#

More men and more vehicles arrived another time, maybe a year ago, maybe more, maybe less. There had been enough time for many of those in the lines to die. The Green Shirts had brought nothing but death and taken nothing but blood from children who were no longer here. The men didn't listen. Laughing Boy watched from the tree on the hill as they worked. They wore clothes like him, dirty shirts and dusty trousers. They wore the sign of the cross but he never saw them pray. Other children gathered behind him, ignoring the women, watching from the safety of the hill, whispering, staring, pulling at his shirt, asking him questions they thought he could answer. Wide-eyed and staring, hushed whispers and hunched shoulders. He strode into the sun and slid down the hill, dirt swelling up behind him like the parachutes that had once dropped food from the sky.

He picked up a piece of metal and received a smack on the back of the head. He dropped it, looked up and smiled, met a man with a face like his but with the warmth of the village women. He attempted to speak and was hit again, these Religious Men so fixated on their work. In the heavy heat they would remove their red crosses and take off their shirts before once again donning the symbol. He watched the Religious Men each day as they dug and heaved and carried and drove their machines and only ever got on their knees not for God but only to dig.

They were ushered together on the last day they would see these Men of God. The women stood in small groups in the centre of the village, mumbling and whispering to one another. He hated the whispering, the silence of the village. The men had been here since last year, maybe more, maybe less. He took a step forward from his classmates and shouted at the line of red crosses gathered in the centre of the village. He avoided the glare of his mother, which was all she had. He now carried the stick. One man said some words, looked at his friends and smiled before placing his hands on a thin piece of metal sticking out the ground. He twisted a palm-sized silver circle in his hands. He looked at the ground, then looked at the crowd, then looked at the ground, expectantly. Nothing happened.

He carried the girl back to the village. They'd gone too far from home. She wanted to see beyond the Lubaki Pass, said she'd never been as far. He knew she was sick. Most of them were sick. His illness had come last year, long after the Religious Men had visited the village. He was bigger, stronger, had fought it, thought he could take care of her.

He would help her fight it; his experience would make her stronger. It didn't. She collapsed. The smooth skin on the back of her legs warmed his arms, and her soft hair drizzled between his fingers, like cotton from years ago. He felt it between his legs, like when they had fought over rocks by the riverbed and he wrestled her to the ground. Her eyes were closed. He tightened his grip on her flaccid body and broke into a run as the village came into view, the meagre collection of homes casting a skeletal shadow on the horizon.

The new visitors were designated into ranks, like his mother and the council. The Blue Men walked around the village spraying everything with more fluids than they had ever seen from the Religious Men's redundant tap. The younger children followed them, jumping in and out of the spray before realising it was not water. The Yellow Men occupied the area around the huge white tent that had been erected in his absence. This was where they had taken the girl. He asked his mother about numerous others. She tried to slap him on the back of the head. He was too quick, too strong. She would not tell him. He could only sit with the women and the younger children, watching the Yellow Men and Blue Men watch them. Any expression was obscured by their masks, thin eyes blankly staring at the huddled cluster of villagers, impotent and ignorant and passive.

He watched as the Fat White Man spoke his words while shedding a tear. Another man seemed to be his elder and would order the Fat Man to repeat his words. He would shed another tear. A group of tiny children gathered around him, clustered around his feet, looking up in awe. The sunlight gleamed off little bald heads that came up to the Fat Man's knees. He sat on a chair that one of his people had brought. He wore clean white clothes, no coloured overalls or yellows. His elder ordered him to take his cigarettes from his shirt pocket. The Fat Man had placed them on the bonnet of their huge white car. They were now in Laughing Boy's pocket. The Fat Man had a beard, but not like the Green Shirt from long ago, not dishevelled and untidy like the valley bushes, a short beard, like a crop struggling to sprout. It followed what remained of his jawline beneath his fat neck. A woman combed his hair before he spoke at the machine carried by another man. The children stared at the device. The Fat Man grabbed one of them and placed him on his knee before the elder told him he was finished. The young boy tried to stroke the Fat Man's face. He slapped the child's hand away before getting up and demanding his cigarettes.

They said they were building a school. He knew because he had asked. No one else had asked. She informed everyone, as if she had spoken with the White Men. His mother, leader of the village, who sat on her behind all day and spoke of nothing but men and places she had never known, who let White Men, Religious Men, Yellow and Blue and Green Men come to the village and test them, question them, hurt them, give them useless water, give them useless hope, give them useless men who built useless things, take photos of them, touch them, smile their smiles at them. We are all friends. We are here to help. We are here to care, to provide, to build. You are here to watch, you are here to write, you are here to learn, and you are here for yourselves. The soft white hand patted him on the shoulder. He said nothing.

The younger ones received an education. Three weeks in the building they called a school. Three weeks before the Teacher Man didn't reappear. Twenty little ones sat cross-legged on the concrete floor, staring at the front of the room, waiting for someone to speak to them. They were supposed to have seats. The old women of the village sat comfortably outside their homes. He had watched from the shadow of the water-store, a building that had only ever been used as a toilet, the faint embers from his cigarette betraying his position in the dark. They came in a pack, fat bodies shuffling through the dirt, babbling and squabbling about nothing, worse than the children, emerging from the school with as many chairs as they could carry. Those they didn't use they burnt.

#

The trucks came later. There was no screaming and shouting when the children were dragged from their homes, when they were rounded up in the middle of the village, the women standing impotently, whispering to each other, alone in their world. The children looked expectantly at their mothers, who offered nothing. He looked on from the hill, from the shadows above the village. He had seen them coming, seen the dust forming on the horizon, a motorised cloud roaring down the dirt-track towards the village, three vehicles blending into their surroundings, like him on the hill, suspended in the solitary tree amid its bare branches.

They wore boots. Some wore black caps, shielding eyes from the sun. Some wore gloves. All wore a uniform. No greens or blues or yellows. Clothes like the colour of dirt, like the colours around them, and all just men, like him.

Guns hung loosely around necks and shoulders or were clipped to belts. Others held larger guns with two hands, probing the nose of their weapons into houses, ordering everyone from their homes. These few continued to point their guns in various directions around the village, waiting for a non-existent enemy. He wanted to tell them they didn't need weapons here. They had long been subdued by much lesser means, by counterfeit kindness, by wooden seats and cotton wool balls, by broken water-wells and ditches and by the needles, small and lethal and precise. He dropped out of the tree and made his way off the hill.

He stood motionless, looked ahead. Others clung to each other for comfort or hope or just to stay together, these boys from other villages, young men of his own age holding onto a childhood he had never known. Some cried, some fell to the ground, some looked anxiously for a comforting face, some were bloodied, some beaten. He stood silent and expressionless, the stoic old man of his village. The Soldier Man had been precise. They must be lined up. There must be order. A young one jumped out of line. He was cracked on the back of the head with the butt of a gun and crumpled to the ground. Dirt and dust billowed up beneath his bare feet as the child was dragged away.

They wrote numbers on their arms. He had watched the others. One group were sent with the Soldier Men with guns. Another group were sent to a building like the school in the village. The others, the smaller ones, those who wouldn't stop crying, were reloaded onto a truck. He reached the front of the column. Most of the boys had to be asked for their arm. He looked the Soldier Man in the eye, quickly thrust out a thick dark limb, smiled and offered him a cigarette.

L'ile des Somnambules
CHAD BENTLEY

It starts hazy but cinematic, the way dreams often do. From the darkness a square of light appears before your eyes. Shapes start to push through the glaze until they are filling the space like a cinema screen. You can do nothing but watch.

The opening is a sweeping crane shot of some small island that is both rural and industrious, with the wide, open green skin broken by jagged steel scars, fragments of a shattered industry still somehow burning away. At the edge sits a ferry port, the only complete mechanical monument that can be seen. The rest, working pits and foundries, are scattered, housed in shattered brick edifices, or out in the open, still running but never at work.

No houses can be seen but there are people, a large group of teenagers with nothing to do but skim over their existence on this impossible rock by giving into neo-pagan desires. The fires they lit created a hostile orange glow caught in conflict with the light from the stars, trapping the island in its violence. You see all this as the camera goes to ground and loops with the inhabitants as they run over the course of the island in a dizzying frenzy.

But as is often the case with stories like this, the true focus is on two people apart from the group. The main cut keeps being disturbed by short, sharp jumps to a boy and a girl. At first these cuts have the ferocity of a runaway train but soon they start to slow down and concentrate on the pair more. Whilst they never appear in the same shot, it is clear from the way the cuts between the two of them linger longer that they would end up finding each other somehow.

The girl is tall, her build hidden beneath a large sheepskin coat, dotted with badges and pins in a mixture of punk and new wave styles. Her blonde hair is cut into a bob but swept back from her face. The sides of her scalp are shorn but a thin layer is starting to grow back. From extreme close-ups you see that she has multiple piercings, one on her nose to the right and a vine running up the arch of her left ear. She wears Doc Marten boots and flesh-coloured tights. Each movement she makes is strong and concise, as if terrified of waste. As she climbs the island's rocky outcrops, her hands only come out of her pockets as a last resort to steady her balance, something that only occurs once in all her screen time.

The boy is younger but changing. He has short sandy hair and looks sullen. With his head always looking down, he can't stop moving, despite not seeming to have the energy to move at all. He is dressed in trainers and a tracksuit, at odds with the vibrant, mismatched clothes of everyone else on the island.

At this moment your sight zooms out from the images and you realise you have been watching the events on the island on your TV screen. You are sat on the sofa, legs stretched and arms resting on your stomach. You begin to doubt whether it is a dream or whether you were just falling asleep at the start of the movie.

The room itself is more or less as it should be. Without the confidence of dreaming, which only comes upon waking, you don't notice the differences: the muted colour palette of monochromatic brown, the flaking plaster. Instead, you are only aware of the familiar: the leather sofa angled parallel to the television, the swirling-patterned carpet, the awkward space of the room.

A memory comes back to you during a quiet moment in the film.

You are standing outside an upstairs room with a person you can't quite place but know intimately. The room itself could have been an attic or a bedroom, possibly both. If it wasn't for a set of foreboding beams on the ceiling and a bristling layer of dust it would have been a little boy's colourful room. Blue walls and a shaggy carpet, with smooth wooden furniture topped with toys. There was a long, wooden bench in the middle of the room. Around the room are scattered piles of notebooks and you are looking for a specific one.

You hover in the doorway chatting jovially but with a tense undercurrent. You share concerns of something… eerie. It was clear you had been spooked but were not sure by what; some vague feelings of a hand on the shoulder in an empty room, angry whispers following you. Perhaps the notebooks would help in some way? You enter, switching the conversation to one about old school days in order to distract yourselves, but there is still something chilling the spaces between words. You focus on wiping dust away from notebooks and attempting to read the first page but none seem to fit. You are so engrossed you don't notice the ceiling start to choke, spitting plaster and dust towards you.

On the island, the girl and the boy, now older, finally meet in the ferry port. The corroding purples and reds of the metal structure creates a stage, hinging between the two expanses of sea and grass. They are shouting, and whilst you cannot understand the words, you know exactly what they mean. They start to climb the rigging towards the crane. Her hair has come loose and is dancing around her face; his cheeks are starting to bruise from screaming. The camera angles are art house cinema but the escalations of the emotional clashes are pure soap opera.

You aren't alone in the house; your parents are busying themselves around you. Your mother tells you about her day as she tidies and your father is behind you somewhere, occasionally making his presence known by grunting and by his increasingly heavy footsteps.

Around you, the usual motifs of your nightmares have found a place in the room. On the floor beside the coffee table are a cluster of spiders. You look away, but as soon as you look back they have been torn apart, leaving a clutter of tiny limbs and almost invisible pools of blood. Was that you? You don't know what you are more disgusted by, the spiders themselves or your own desire to have been their destroyer.

And then there is the ghost of the house, whom you are aware of like an inconvenient truth. You have even given him a name that you cannot remember, like something you would call the devil. There is also your father and his walk. You hear his footsteps grow heavier and less rhythmic. You can see his frame crumbling lower and his skin becoming more like the plaster on the walls. You try to ignore the rest of it, but parental affliction always gets under your skin.

Amidst the blur of noise, one line keeps standing out. *You should see the scars on his arse*, your mother keeps saying in fits of shrill laughter. You do not know who she means. As you turn away from her laughter, you notice the walls are closer together.

Back on the island the two loners are still in the ferry port, but time has clearly passed. The wind has died down and they are sitting on top of the crane. Held in a deep focus shot, they are at peace with the island but not with each other. The stillness of the camera and the calm setting are contradicted by their restless bodies. She is constantly moving and re-pinning the badges on her coat; he is swinging his legs in a marching rhythm, almost daring his body to slip off the scaffolding. Every time they reach out to hold one another they can only manage a few seconds before their faces bustle up in anguish and they snatch their bodies back.

It is only when the camera switches to an arcing shot around the couple that you finally appreciate the scope of the emptiness around the island and you are hit by the pervading feeling of being trapped by the infinite. You shudder.

You're searching more frantically for the notebook, with plaster and wood falling faster onto your heads. Each notebook opened is the wrong one, but the more you open the more you realise you don't know what you are looking for. Each one contains an oddly familiar scrawl censored by further layers of dust. The ceiling is choking louder now; whatever the blockage is will soon be spat out onto your heads.

You turn to leave, ready to give up, but there is a thing in the doorway – the something 'eerie' that you still can't fathom. Behind you, the beams collapse. You turn to scream but it is too late. The room is filled with rubble, covered in a thick layer of dust. The other has vanished. The thing from the doorway places a hand on your shoulder; you feel its jagged breath cut into your neck. You hear it smile. It has won.

At this point you decide to watch the film in consolation.

The exchanges between the lovers are getting more intense. The jump cuts became more hazardous, completely abandoning any linear narrative flow. Out on the island they are happy, shown walking hand in hand over the grasslands. If it wasn't for the odd angles and the speed of changes it would have been peaceful. These were edited together with the pair becoming enemies in the intimacy of a house, the exterior so far unseen. Here, you watch the boy pull apart a crumpled windshield with his bare hands while the girl tears piercings from her face in an extreme close-up. In the next cut they start throwing rocks, or a rock. It is here the timeline splits and you are no longer only watching one film.

Your mother starts chastising you for your viewing choice so close to bedtime. Arguing against this, you start telling her about the artistic merit of the film. That, of these two characters, one was always destined to kill the other, it just doesn't matter which. The film makes you watch each scenario, each death, makes you feel the pain and the loss twice over. Like all nightmares and car crashes it won't let you look away. Instead, it forces you to experience it from every agonising angle.

As you tell her this, the images of the film provide corroboration. The cuts become chaotic, whipping between timelines like the pages of a book left out in a storm. She is screaming. He is screaming. He throws the rock. She throws it. Suddenly they are in a bath. It wasn't where they had thrown the rock but it was where the impact will be felt. At this stage the chaotic nature of the timelines become too much as the two threads abandon each other, each taking up a portion of the screen, fighting for space.

In one scene she cradles his body in her arms, the faintest hint of blood bubbling from his forehead, dispersing into the water of the bath. Her face is devastation. The camera does not know where to turn; it tries to hide in the corners of the room, all the while keeping its focus locked solely on her, steadily zooming in on her face. The intensity of it breaks through the safety of the screen, overwhelming you in her agony.

On the other side he is quiet. The physical impact on her had been oddly powerful, causing her body to break open.

He sits in the water, easing her flesh from her bones. As she screams at her loss in one scene, he pulls her organs from her body in the other, rearranging them in a bath of her blood. He left no small space unfilled. It had become like some kind of grotesque modern art to him. The camera shows all of this in an unflinchingly still top shot.

At this moment, consciousness creeps up on you and you are awake. You are old enough that you should be able to roll back to sleep but you can't. Instead, you get out of bed and start to cross the house, supposing that you are never too old for the comfort of parents.

You cross the living room to open your parents' door but the dust-covered handle comes off in your hand. You reach the light switch beside the door and turn it on. The first thing you notice is the plaster flaking off the walls and the muted brown colours. On the floor you see the legs of spiders scattered around and behind you stands a figure your mind cannot quite explain. Next to him is a body that you know intimately but cannot place. You notice that the walls seem closer together and on the TV there are only two overlapping squares of static.

You wake up. Finally free from the vestiges of sleep, you swing your legs out of bed and place your feet on the cold corrugated metal… You have been lying on a sheet in a ferry port. Beyond you rests an expanse of grass interrupted only by vague fragments of industry. Behind you is only sea. You feel yourself start to shake.

At the furthest point of the island your vision fractures into two squares of shattered light. To the right you can make out a girl, and to the left, a boy. They are flickering. From somewhere you can hear the sounds of a party. You are still shaking despite feeling a hand rest on your shoulder and jagged breath cut into your neck. You see a smile.

You clench your eyes shut, afraid reality has turned against you. There is a light behind your eyelids like a cinema screen. Vague shapes are starting to push through and fill the space.

You can do nothing but watch.

An Evening Out
ASHA KRISHNA

So what do you do?

A simple question for anyone but this mum. She dreaded it the most.

Sitting in that dimly lit room with six other mums, she was filled with trepidation. Is this worth it? Will I ever fit in?

Despite living in the provincial little English village for the last five years, she had always felt like an outsider. She recalled, with a chuckle, opening the door to a Jehovah's Witness one time. Her caramel skin and dark hair was enough to shock him into silence and make him disappear, but not before shoving a pamphlet into her hand.

Well, not that she had made much attempt to socialise. Her cultural differences had marked her out as different in the village anyway. She did not feel comfortable approaching the community, and they seemed distant too.

She never cared before. She cared now. Her daughter, Mia, had just started at the village school. Unlike her, the little girl did not carry that baggage of cultural consciousness. A cheerful child, she was already forging friendships in class.

Standing outside at the school gate every day, the mums were getting acquainted with each other. But now they wanted to form a bond of their own, to complement this relationship between their children.

And so came an invitation from a mum, Julie, calling the group over to her place for drinks and nibbles – *'after the kids were tucked in and the husbands got in'*, the invite read.

She knew a bit about the 'mummy gang' – Julie the high-flying banker and meticulous planner; Zoe, the glamourous fashion designer mum; Jenny the superwoman, reminding others what the child had to bring into school, while juggling numbers as an accountant.

Knocking at the door, she could not remember the last time she went off on her own for an evening out. Not since her wedding surely. Ravi and she always socialised as a couple, but after having the kids, night outs were completely ruled out. But there was a time when things were different... those crazy night shifts rounded off with a stopover at a takeaway shop... it seemed like such a lifetime ago.

The door was opened and she was greeted by a cheerful, made-up face.

'There you are! We were wondering about you. Did you find the place all right?' Julie moved aside to let her in.

Ashamed to admit that she got lost, despite the nagging satnav and having to circle around twice before she got into the right lane, she just nodded.

As she walked into the living room, the others were settling into comfortable chairs with drinks in their hands. The centre table was neatly laid out with nibbles and beverages.

'What can I get you to drink? I have wine, beer.'

'Anything non-alcoholic?'

'I'm sure there is orange juice in the fridge. Sorry, darling, didn't realise you were teetotal.'

'Thanks.'

Looking at other mums in their smart outfits and evening make-up, she subconsciously ran a hand over her defiant hair. She had barely managed to dab some foundation and lipstick on before stepping out of the chaos of the evening dinner. While the other mums had managed to tuck their kids in by seven, hers were still up as she left the house, leaving Ravi in charge. She tried not to think about it as she focussed on the moment.

Outside the window, fog was moving in, but inside it was warm and cosy: a circle of inviting sofas and comfy chairs, Classic FM playing softly in the background. Clearly, it was an attempt at a welcoming ambience, designed to make the guests feel comfortable. The mum felt as though she was in the waiting room, about to be called in for an interview.

After few spurts of small talk, conversations seemed to stretch out, with lengthy pauses. Newly acquainted, the mums, after all, did not have a shared history yet.

'Hi, everyone.' Everyone looked up towards Julie.

'Why don't we start with introducing ourselves and what we do?'

The mum was a bit surprised and disconcerted. Will she have to prove herself, instead of just easing herself in, unnoticed? There was a time when she would have jumped at a chance like this, making the right sounds, showing off, but not anymore. She did not want to talk about her work.

She planned to stick to the story of a stay-at-home mother. She could not take any questions about her past. Not tonight.

As the women started talking about what they did, the mum felt anxious and even more out of place. Her heart was beating fast as the introductions were moving around.

It was her turn. 'I am a stay-at-home mother and have lived in the village for five years.'

The room felt oddly subdued. Everyone else had gone on and on about their work, the driving force, how it defined them. In comparison to that, the one-liner sounded as hollow as forced laughter.

As though prompting her, Julie asked her what she did. But for the mum, it felt as though the questioning stares burned into her skin, ready to pass judgement on her next word.

'I came to this country to study. When I met my future husband, I decided to stop.' It was not entirely true, but at least it would stop a lot of questions.

'Oh! What did you study?'

'Medicine.'

Memories of that night shift still haunted her. It was a busy Saturday at the ward and news of a motorway pileup had just come in. The hospital was short-staffed already. She was the only junior registrar on the team that night. As the patients were wheeled in, a couple tugged at her white coat, begging her to save their little girl. Swamped with so many casualties, she had just made it to the critically injured child.

She tried her best to revive her, but it was too late. She couldn't help feeling that if only she'd got to her earlier, without wading through the other critically injured, she could have saved this girl's life.

The distraught parents, caught up in grief and shock, made an official complaint against her, but she was cleared of any negligence. However, she couldn't bring herself to go back on the ward. Her surgeon husband, Ravi, though sympathetic, found it difficult to reach out to her due to his forthright demeanour.

What is the point of being a doctor if you cannot save a life? The mother's wail constantly reverberated in her ears.

It didn't help that she was pressed to answer questions back home about her decision to quit medicine. *All that money spent on your education? Down the drain?* her parents asked. She knew she had disappointed them, made them lose face in the community. *A doctor who just gave it all up. What a waste!* There were constant hints and 'advice' from friends and relatives, urging her to think about going back. *You have invested too much in it to give it up*, and *Why? For something that was not your fault?*

But she couldn't summon that guileless devotion for the profession anymore. Something snapped in her at the thought of working in a system that was failing its people. The desolate look in the parents' eyes as they watched their child slip away haunted her dreams. Her thoughts were like the flat line on the heart monitor – constant and futile – as she sat by the window for hours, staring into oblivion.

And then, she found out she was pregnant.

Taking this as a cue, Ravi moved them to the countryside, away from the jabs of prying relatives.

The pregnancy wasn't easy, and it helped that she was off work. Throughout the nine-month period, there was a lingering fear of a curse casting its shadow. Anxiously, she kept waiting for that tiny blip, anything to suggest an anomaly.

The delivery was smooth but transformed her completely. Familial rejection and a keen sense of failure had turned her into a social recluse, redefining her as a parent rather than an individual. Ravi worked long hours but she didn't mind, enjoying her time with little Mia. Her baby boy followed soon after and she quickly realised that looking after a toddler and an infant consumed all her time.

But she seemed content, revelling in this domesticity, not having to engage with the outside world and its challenges. She preferred taking the kids to quiet parks rather than toddler groups.

But now, she had to get back into the social circuit for the sake of her little darling, to pave her way into the community. It was hard to ignore those debilitating thoughts of inadequacy and anxiety. Plus, she didn't think she had anything in common with the other mums. An Asian, unemployed, reclusive mum did seem like a misfit in this group of inclusive, career-driven, socially active mothers.

But she knew she would have to let them in, maybe just a little.

'I was training to be a doctor but I gave it up.'

'Oh wow. Motherhood intervened?' said Julie, playing with a strand of hair.

She let that go and just smiled in return. *Let them think what they want.* She didn't want to clarify or defend her decision. She had done enough of that already.

But her silence seemed to cry out. Of squirming reasons trapped in a water bubble.

Julie blurted out: 'Way back as young, reckless professionals, Martin and I got carried away and bought a four-bedroom house on the outskirts of London. It didn't bother us that it was too big and came with a fat mortgage. Martin earned well and we always had friends over. One day, he came home saying he'd lost his job. My salary wasn't enough. Overnight, all our friends disappeared. The house was repossessed. That's when we decided to move to the village and make a fresh start.'

The mum looked up with her eyes wide. Was Julie drunk? This was definitely not the meticulous planner she knew.

The shock revelation was still hanging in the air. Julie broke the silence.

'Sorry. Didn't mean to spit it out. But glad I did. It feels much better. So now that Mia is at school and your boy will join her soon, do you plan to get back to work eventually?'

Intense revelation one minute, small talk the next. Either the woman was bipolar or she was a terrific hostess, the medic mum thought to herself.

'I do not want to go back to medicine. That's a closed chapter for me.'

'I know the feeling. It's amazing how we strive to get there and then suddenly it doesn't seem worth it after all,' said Zoe as she shifted in her chair.

'As a foster child, I always dreamt of a family of my own. I spent a long time looking for that perfect partner to make it happen. I met Ken through my clients and saw him as the one. Imagine my excitement when he proposed to me saying he shared my dream of the perfect family too. One day, I walked into a coffee shop. He was sitting there with my best friend, barely keeping his hands off her.' Zoe broke off, gulping down the contents of her glass.

'But you… didn't walk out?' Julie asked.

'No. He begged me, crying his heart out that it was a mistake, *a one-off*. I've seen what happens to kids when parents separate. I didn't want that for my children. They adore him, and keeping him away will devastate them. I decided to keep quiet and let things be. But then the built-up frustration led to suicidal thoughts. I've been seeing a counsellor to sort it out.' She lifted the glass to her lips, realised it was empty and put it down.

In the quiet of the room, it was as though all the ghosts were walking out of the shadows. The dim light seemed to draw out confidences, and the drink was lowering inhibitions.

The mum felt something shift within her. A pinprick piercing through the water bubble, letting out a trickle. Taking a deep breath, she said: 'Let me start again. I'm Meena. As a junior doctor, I watched a little girl die in front of my eyes. All because I couldn't reach her in time. A beautiful life was snuffed out because the system and I failed her. I cannot bear wearing the hospital scrubs again. My family doesn't understand it and we moved away because of that. I've been told it wasn't my fault, but every time I look in the mirror, a failure stares back at me.'

'Believe me when I say I know,' said Jenny, the supermum.

'I have an older daughter, Delia, tucked away in a residential school. She was diagnosed with poor brain development when she was a year old. Initially, my husband and I thought we could do it – care for her ourselves. But then, after ten years, on the verge of a breakdown, we gave in and sent her away. We wanted another baby to make up for Delia but couldn't run the risk. We adopted Jill, now in the same class as your little ones.'

'We see Delia every weekend. But each time, it reminds me what a pathetic mother I am.'

#

Cultural barrier… social image… such myths. Scratch it a little, and beneath it they were all made of the same stuff. Women who had made their choices. No need to impress each other, they did it just by being upfront about it.

Finally, after years of living in the cocoon she had built around her, Meena sensed a metaphorical crack, a tiny head pushing its way out, to reach out to the world beyond.

Perhaps, when they meet at the gate tomorrow, the façade will be back in place. But for now, they were warming up to each other under the blanket of shared confidences.

Berated by her friends and family, and now sitting around with this bunch of mums, Meena somehow felt at home.

The Tiny Path
SIMON BLAND

I was the kind of child who put my mother on the edge – the teeth-gritting, hair-tearing wall-punching edge.

'Hold my hand, Timmy. Don't pull, it's *dangerous*… come away from the kerb!'

If there was traffic, I would veer towards cars. She tried to protect me. She hated the exposure of my lungs to thick, belching exhaust fumes, and she'd try to keep me as far away from the road as possible, but I would pull against her, extricate my fingers from hers. I'd run when told not to, or dawdle when she was in a desperate hurry. But she loved me with the passion of a ravenous bear.

Cars were her biggest fear, and my tantrums, while strapped in the back of our own, didn't help. I'd kick hard, like a goat, as she drove. I knew she could feel my feet beating against the back of her seat to alert her to my emergency. A dinosaur or a mini-cheddar might have slipped out of my hand as we bumped over potholes.

It was the noise that got to her – my five-year-old screams – and although I can barely remember all this, I have a sense of it, a keen sense of the anxiety I caused. That, and both she and my father gave detailed accounts over the dinner table of how I used to be. Things did get better – but for a peculiar reason.

It was a grey half-term before the summer holidays. The previous day had been fun. She'd got some air-dry clay and we'd made dragons with the pointy ends of barbecue sticks for teeth. But today it took a while for her to get out of bed. Her eyes didn't seem to open properly, and my five-year-old inclination was, of course, to aggravate her. That's what children do.

The trip for groceries hadn't been a success. I'd wanted a packet of sweets; she said no. I filled my lungs and screamed; I lay flat on the shop floor and refused to get up.

An elderly woman walked past and tutted. 'Another one who can't control 'em.'

The cashier sniffed and lifted her eyebrows with disdain. The people in the queue were clearly irritated. Mummy left the groceries and picked me up as I fought back with every bit of strength I had. I bit, pulled her hair and kicked. It was a while before she could get me to the car and strap me in, but as soon as she had, I fought my way out of the seat belt.

She started taking strange long breaths as I played with the interior light, and then she said: 'I'll allow you to have the sweets if you *calm down* so I can drive home safely.'

The queue was just as long where the contents of our abandoned shopping basket were now being emptied by a weary-looking shop assistant and placed back on the shelves, but I was getting my sweets, a sherbet lolly dip and some mints. There was a moment before she started the car again – she had a tissue and was blowing her nose. 'Tim, I just can't do this anymore. I've had enough. I'm tired of fighting.'

I looked at the bright red lolly and poked it into the yellow powder. She didn't say anything else but started the engine and began to drive.

'Why are we stopping, Mummy?' I'd been so distracted by the sherbet stuff I'd never tasted before that it was a while before I noticed we were nowhere near home but instead just out of town. She pulled into a lay-by.

'What's the matter, Mummy?' It looked like she was shaking. Her head was bent against the steering wheel. She then slowly straightened, took more of the strange breaths, got out and unstrapped me.

'Let's just go for a walk. I need some fresh air.' There was a sound in her voice, a madness that made me curious.

Away from the road it was quiet. The lemony smell of the sherbet on my fingers mixed with the fresh-smelling earth and fallen leaves. Beyond the lay-by was a thicket of trees. We made our way through them, and there was the distant sound of a stream below an abrupt cliff edge.

'Don't touch that!' She pulled me away as I was just about to poke a mushroom. 'It's *Amanita* something or other,' she murmured. 'Destroying angel… it's on our calendar… it's deadly, Tim, so don't go near it.'

We both crouched close. It had a smooth disk-like cap with a dainty skirt around the stalk. I badly wanted to feel the smooth white surface.

'Why's it deadly, Mummy?'

'Because it's poisonous, like if a snake's venom got into you. It's very bad, fatal…'

'What's fatal?'

There was a sound behind us. 'Hello, there.'

My mother jumped at the voice. I went to reach, to touch the fungi, when I saw a man.

'Is that your son?'

My mother's hand was tight around my own. His brown close-set eyes peered down at me. I felt as small as the mushroom.

'What are you doing here?' She was pretending to be casual. She said it lightly but I sensed her uneasiness.

'Just taking a walk, taking a shortcut.'

His tone was friendly, but he smiled in a way that seemed like he was very pleased with himself. He had his hands deep in the pockets of his jeans, but when he pulled one of them out, I noticed how badly bitten his nails were, almost like there were just ridges of skin. I tried to reach for that smooth mushroom at my feet.

'…we were looking for his toy.'

At this, I felt the need to correct her. 'I haven't—'

But she squeezed my hand so painfully tight, I gasped. That smooth white skin was just beyond my fingertips. The scent of the earth was heady and rich.

The man came nearer. It seemed like they knew each other, although they didn't refer to one another by name. There was a familiarity that I didn't understand. He casually wandered close to the cliff edge, which was a few steps away.

'Quite a drop, isn't it?' He glanced back, his eyes on me for a second.

'He dropped his dinosaur…'

I was about to correct her when she let go of my hand, and for that moment everything seemed to slow down.

'It's in the car,' I said, and with this, his head slowly turned. He went to straighten himself and step away from the cliff edge, but she gave him a kick. I could tell how hard it was from the sound. She tripped back, knocking me over, and my view of the toadstool was twisted. There was a wail, and then a crack, like a branch or maybe the impact of bone against rock.

'Where did he go?' She didn't reply but helped me up and walked to the edge, where he'd been. She crouched like we did over the deadly mushroom.

'Mummy…?'

She turned, took a breath, and said lightly, 'Do you need to pee?' She didn't sound angry anymore. She sounded relaxed. 'Are you OK, darling? I bet you're thirsty.'

'What happened to that man?'

'I don't know, he just went.'

'But…'

'I think you should have a pee before we get in the car.'

It was difficult for me to comprehend her calmness, so I didn't say anything. She helped me down with my trousers and I obediently let out a jet at the base of a tree.

'It's nice to get out, isn't it?' She opened the car and I got in. I didn't scream this time.

#

A storm broke on the afternoon we'd stopped in the lay-by. Just before we left for home, as I was being strapped in, a few pats of water splashed on her woollen cardigan, but she didn't seem bothered at all. In fact, she appeared quite cheerful and switched the radio on.

There was a morbid fear brewing within me that my mother was bad, but also a doubt about what I'd seen. A very voluntary doubt. But still, I had to dig.

'Mummy, did you push that man?'

'Of course not!' She said it warmly. 'He just went.' By now the windscreen wipers were swishing frantically. She started humming.

'Went where, Mummy?'

'Oh, there's a tiny path. Didn't you see it, darling? He went that way.'

The tiny path. I wanted to see this tiny path, like it was magic.

I was afraid of the storm that night. It reminded me of her anger – her old anger – it made me think of the countless times she would put a meal before me that she'd spent an hour preparing and I would whine, complain and then seal my lips. Or the times we'd nearly had an accident because she was blindly scraping about, one arm behind her and one on the steering wheel, to recover a toy and stop my screaming. There was also the occasion I'd drawn over her new quilt and bedroom walls in felt pen. It never came out.

She wore her anger from one incident to the next like a leaden cloak.

But now it was as if this fury had been exchanged with the storm outside. She was calm while the weather growled and raged.

'I'm scared, Daddy.' I'd gone into their bedroom. The shower stopped in the bathroom, where I could now hear my mother humming the tune we'd just heard on the radio.

'If you kick someone over a cliff, will it hurt?' I asked him as he led me back to my room, explaining to him that Mummy had kicked someone. I'm not sure why it came out, but bedtime fairy tales, enveloped by night, create alternative possibilities. The world seems different. It felt safe to ask.

'Yes, it would hurt.' He tucked me in and gave me a kiss.

'What's this?' My mother's hair was wet. She was wrapped in a towel.

I didn't want Daddy to tell her but he did. He seemed a bit confused. 'Apparently you *kicked* someone over a cliff?'

'Oh.' Mummy sat at the corner of the bed and squeezed my foot through the duvet. 'I think you had a dream while you were in the car. You woke up saying you wanted to see a tiny path.'

That was enough for me. They were happy. *We* were happy. I didn't fight with her as much, at all even. There was a certainty now in my mother that made me accept her rules. Things felt better after that day and what *I thought* I saw or dreamt seemed to fade.

Some weeks later, I overheard them talking, but I was too young to make any connection. I'd got out of bed to ask for a cup of water. They were sitting in the kitchen, looking at an article in the local paper. I hung back at the door.

'His body was found after the flood. It was him,' my father said. 'For once a story that isn't so tragic.'

My mother put her hand on his. 'There wouldn't be an "us" if he'd got what he wanted,' and she said more darkly, 'I'd hardly left school. He pestered me, joked that he was possessive…'

'He stalked you… I'm surprised he hasn't bothered you since.'

She was quiet for a while, then, 'He did rear his ugly head now and then.'

'What?'

'He'd appear out of nowhere, in a car park or… just anywhere. Sometimes when I was walking home he'd cross my path…' She said it casually, without the kind of anxiety I was used to. My father, on the other hand, looked unsettled.

'You never told me this.'

'Sometimes a problem shared isn't halved to me. Two people know about it. I didn't want it to poison us. Anyway, it stopped by the time we had Timmy, or I would've gone to the police. Sometimes I wonder if he'd seen me with a baby and let it go, but he went to prison, didn't he?'

'You didn't see him because he was locked up for harming someone else and doing the same stuff he did to you.'

'Just think, if I hadn't got away, there'd be no us, no Tim… *Timmy*!'

She put her hand over her mouth as I emerged from the door. 'Can I have some water, please?'

#

Fifteen years later my head was now full of plans for university. It was a Saturday and I was rooting around, trying to find a match or a lighter. I needed a smoke.

My mother had been clearing stuff out and rearranging where things were stored. They were having an attic conversion. There was now a bundle of old notepads in the kitchen drawer. It wasn't looking likely there'd be a lighter. I doubtfully pulled out the recipes scribbled for dandelion wine and cider vinegar when a newspaper clipping slipped to the floor. I picked it up, giving it little attention, pushed it to one side, impatient for nicotine, and found a small envelope of matches from the local Chinese takeaway. They were ancient, with just three strikes left. I began to roll some tobacco when my gaze fell on the grocery bag still unpacked on the counter. My mother would often go shopping, become distracted by something, and forget to unpack everything. She was now chatting away on the phone upstairs.

There was a brown paper bag amongst the shopping. I untwisted the corners. Smooth white mushrooms were inside. It wasn't something I would normally do, but I held the bag to my face and inhaled. It was that time of year again, the best foraging time. I struck the match, expecting it to be damp, but it lit, and noticing there didn't seem to be a recipe on either side of the scrap of newspaper, I wandered into the garden, wondering at its significance.

There was an inset photo of a man's face and a larger one of a place. The picture had been taken 'after the storm', as the caption described it. Or, more specifically, 'the deadly cliff, after the storm'. There were specks of white on the ground, I peered closer at the black and white article, right into the grain in the image, and picked out the shape of a mushroom. A white fleck, a cipher in the pattern.

Perhaps if they hadn't been left in the kitchen, if I hadn't caught a whiff of that earthy smell, it would have been forgotten forever. It took three things to trigger the memory, I think: the smell, the sight of his beady close eyes and the place itself. If all three hadn't been there, I probably wouldn't have remembered.

Then I saw her. A flash of memory.

It was the way someone would kick a door. Hard with the heel. Direct. In the exact right spot to break a lock. My smoke had gone out. I threw it away, grabbed my bike and pedalled straight to the lay-by.

There was a fence now, beyond the trees, to prevent people getting too close to the edge, but it was now bent and rusted. As I squeezed through a wider gap, I noticed at the foot of a beech, entangled in the roots, a couple of those white killer mushrooms.

He dropped his dinosaur.

I wondered if I imagined her saying that, and her boot on the seat of his faded Levi's, and that sharp thump.

I wondered if it was me.

For a moment I questioned if she'd taken me there in a fit of maternal rage to throw me over – I was by all accounts a little shit at that age. I fought to remember, to tease back any sensation.

Sitting right on the edge now, at the highest point I could find, I got a pinch of tobacco and rolled another cigarette. I *had* been difficult. I kind of knew it. She'd start with love, and then I'd wind her up.

I blew a plume of smoke out and listened. It was quiet, like it was then – barely a passing car. She got away with murder, and in a manner of speaking, I did as well. I probably pushed her to do it. But she never hurt me. Not once. And every day, almost every moment of every day, she'd give me a big fat hug and tell me how much she loved me.

That afternoon she'd been tested, like any other. She'd stopped in the lay-by because I'd got out of my seat. It was dangerous. We'd taken a walk, and then afterwards I remember her helping me pee against a tree.

But most of all, I remember how tightly she held my hand when he came along.

The Pink Feather Boa Incident
KATHERINE HETZEL

'Excuse me? I think you dropped something?'

Paul turned towards the man who'd stopped him and half smiled, half frowned at the pink feather being held out to him. 'Nope, not me.'

'Are you sure, Paul? It is Paul, isn't it?'

The man was persistent, the voice vaguely familiar, but he couldn't place it. 'Do I know you?'

It was Amelie who recognised him. Oh, there was now a paunch, and thinning hair, but the face was etched onto her memory, even if Paul didn't remember…

'We were students together.' The man stepped closer, pocketing the feather. 'Business Studies and Finance, about… twenty-five years ago?'

Twenty-seven, Amelie whispered, but Paul didn't listen. He didn't listen to her very much at all these days.

'Oh, right.' Paul frowned. 'I'm sorry, I don't remember you.'

The stranger's face darkened momentarily. 'Richard. Richard Fraser.'

'Richard. How are you doing?' He had no idea who this man was, whether he'd studied with him or not, but he shook hands with him anyway.

Amelie winced at the contact.

'Not as well as you, it seems.' Richard nodded towards the glass and steel building in whose shadow they stood. Three-foot-high letters above the entrance spelled out 'Hemming Finance'.

Paul shrugged. 'I worked hard, got lucky a few times.'

'Yeah, looks like it.'

Was there a hint of jealousy wrapped around those words? If so, Paul chose to ignore it.

'Always said you'd go far. Not like me. Saw the article in *Hello*, by the way. What was it they voted you? Finance wizard and most eligible bachelor of the decade, wasn't it? I'm pleased for you.'

Amelie noticed that Richard's smile didn't seem to reach his eyes, and she shuddered.

Paul glanced at his Rolex, keen to get on, get away from this man who appeared to know an awful lot about him but was still a stranger. 'Thanks. Look, sorry to cut this short, but I have a ten o'clock meeting. Nice to see you again, Richard. All the best.' He turned away, mind already on the job, and walked towards his workplace.

'Yeah, you too. Perhaps we can meet up sometime? Have a proper catch-up?' Richard called after him. 'Bring Amelie and–'

The door swung shut behind Paul, cutting off the rest.

#

Two days later, the first envelope arrived.

'Excuse me. Mr Hemming?'

Paul glanced up from the analysis of Barty Leminster's holdings. 'Yes?'

Cecile stepped quickly towards the desk. 'This just arrived. Marked confidential.'

He gestured towards the in-tray. 'Why do they bother? Leave it, I'll check it in a bit.'

Ten minutes after Cecile left, he signed off Barty's documents – how much gold could one man need? – and reached for the letter. It amused him that some of his clients still insisted on sending their paperwork to him personally, as though unaware that their business deals were actually handled by his portfolio managers. But Paul had gotten into the habit of opening all the correspondence marked 'confidential' anyway, because a client whose finances were handled personally, albeit for mere seconds, by Mr Hemming himself, seemed to keep coming back. So Paul opened the envelope and grinned. How much would its contents add to his turnover this time?

At first, he thought it was a joke, that the envelope was empty, but then he caught sight of the feather. He pulled the bright pink thing out and an old dread settled, heavy, in his stomach.

Then he dropped both feather and envelope into the bin.

Three days later, another envelope arrived, identical to the first. Marked confidential. This time, the pink feather was stuck to a small card, on which was written a short message and a phone number.

Amelie owes me, it said.

Paul's gut churned, but for the first time in a long while, he allowed himself to remember…

And then he waited.

For a whole week, his heart raced every time Cecile dropped any post into his in-tray, but there were no more envelopes marked confidential. He began to relax, to think the danger had passed, when the third one arrived.

Inside was a sheet of folded paper and the inevitable pink feather.

Paul peeled the paper open. His chest tightened, he couldn't breathe – but he couldn't stop looking.

Someone had gone to great lengths to mock up the front page of *The Sun*. 'FINANCE FRAUD' screamed the headline, and Amelie's face filled the space underneath.

The photographer had caught her mid-laugh, head thrown back in gleeful abandon, champagne glass in hand;

'It's not a party without champagne, darling!' It had always sounded like a battle cry to Paul...

His breathing easier now, he stroked Amelie's cheek on the page. How unencumbered she'd been, like a bird set free from its cage, the life and soul of every party. No wonder he'd been drawn to her. She'd been everything he wanted to be, instead of the studious young man, trapped and wrapped in numbers and equations that he'd become. Still was, if he was honest.

He remembered perfectly the night the picture had been taken, because Amelie was wearing the bloody pink feather boa, the one she'd picked up for pennies in the flea market that very morning. It had tickled his nose and shed feathers everywhere, but she'd loved it. She'd worn it that evening while she drank gallons of champagne and then wrapped it round the neck of–

'Richard Fraser,' Paul murmured. 'Shit!'

The name hit him with the force of a well-placed punch, winding him afresh as he remembered the balding stranger holding out a pink feather. He crumpled the paper and threw it at the wall, sudden anger burning hot in his chest. THAT Richard? Why the hell hadn't Amelie tipped him off? Or had she tried, and – like normal – he'd ignored her, like he so often did these days? He'd been so careful to keep her out of his new world, allowing her only the rarest of forays back into the bright lights of London nightlife that she used to love so much.

Paul ran a hand over his face, trying to think.

Twenty-seven years ago, Richard Fraser had scared them. He'd started hanging round Paul in the last year of uni in a vain attempt to pick up enough information to avoid a third degree from the student most likely to gain a first. He'd met Amelie purely by chance when she'd decided to celebrate graduation early. For a while Paul had thought everything would be all right, watching from a distance as Amelie flirted with Richard but kept him at arm's length.

But Richard had been persistent. The… what to call it? Affair? Infatuation? Paul wasn't sure. Whatever formed the root of the connection that Amelie and Richard had, it continued to grow long after the proper graduation ceremony, right up to the night of what Paul referred to as The Pink Feather Boa Incident. He couldn't remember all the details – perhaps he'd deliberately blocked them from his memory – but he knew that Richard had got too close that night and threatened to tear Amelie's world apart. Sensible Paul had come to the rescue, forced her to leave the club, the unpaid-for champagne – and Richard Fraser – behind.

The recent accidental meeting, the feathers in the envelopes; everything stemmed from that night. Paul was certain of it. He was certain of something else, too. Having successfully avoided Amelie for the longest period of time to date, he was going to have to talk to her about Richard. And soon.

#

'We can't let him ruin everything I've worked for and built because of you.' Paul knew that would hurt Amelie, but he didn't feel like holding back. She was fully aware that she embarrassed him, always had been. She'd done her best to live with the restrictions he placed on her, and he was grateful for that. Things had been going well recently, since he hadn't seen so much of her.

But now, Richard threatened everything. He was too large a pebble to be chucked into what had been a still pond; the ripples of potential consequence were simply too big to ignore.

'We have to do something,' Paul said.

Amelie spoke for the first time. 'Well, I started this. I suppose I ought to finish it.'

Finish it? Paul frowned. 'What?'

'We'll have to get rid of him.'

The certainty in her voice sent a trickle of fear down Paul's spine. 'What do you mean?' And yet deep down he knew full well, had suspected what Amelie the confident, Amelie the strong, Amelie the uninhibited, would suggest. 'Not…? I can't! What if–'

Amelie sighed. 'I know you can't. Why don't you stick to your numbers and leave dealing with Richard to me? Hmm?'

At that moment, he both loved and hated her in equal measure. Loved her for being capable of doing what he was too weak to do himself. Hated her for the same reason. But could he let go of the situation, allow her to take control? The thought of what he could lose if Richard's mock newspaper headlines ever hit the real tabloids decided him. Reluctant, but secretly relieved, Paul nodded.

'I'd better get on, then.' Amelie grinned and stretched in that catlike way she had, sending a shiver of anticipation down Paul's spine. 'You said there was a phone number?'

The razor slid easily over Amelie's skin and she followed it with her hand, checking for stray hairs. It would be no good snagging her stockings as soon as she put them on. Satisfied with a job well done, she rose from the water –

'Like Venus from the waves,' she murmured.

– and patted herself dry as the bubbles and stubble drained away.

She applied the makeup carefully, camouflaging the telltale signs that she wasn't twenty-one any more. A slick of lipstick to finish and –

'Perfect.' She blew a kiss at her reflection and laughed. How long had it been since she'd done this? She was going to savour every second of it.

Richard was waiting at the bar when Amelie arrived. She saw his eyes widen and heard his low whistle as she sashayed towards him, the simple but oh-so-elegant silk wrap dress clinging to her body and cool against her skin, her slingback heels the perfect height to emphasise her shapely calves. She'd been careful not to overdo things, of course. To show him that she wasn't the same flighty creature she'd been then, but still someone he could desire.

'Hello, Richard.'

'Amelie. I didn't think you'd come.'

He offered champagne and she sipped it slowly, keeping him waiting, aware of the power she still held over him. Maybe that's why she hadn't given him up all those years ago. Well, not until Paul had forced her to. She'd always loved feeling powerful. With a jolt, she realised that she and Paul were more alike than either of them had ever realised…

'I was in two minds for a while,' she said eventually. 'But Paul agreed it was for the best. He sent you this.' She pulled the brown envelope from her clutch bag, careful not to pull out the other thing with it, and held it out. Richard looked puzzled, so she explained. 'It's payback for all the champagne I drank that night. I think you'll find he's been most generous. Debt paid.'

She watched as Richard checked the contents before slipping the envelope into his pocket.

'I thought Paul' – Richard laid a subtle emphasis on the name – 'would have given more to keep your… association with him under wraps.' His eyes ran over her body while his tongue ran over his lips.

Amelie smiled. She'd known that money wouldn't be enough to ensure there were no further repercussions. Richard's undisguised and years-old unfulfilled lust would play right into her hands. She dropped a hand onto his thigh. 'I seem to remember I left you before things could get… interesting,' she purred. 'Shall we allow ourselves an interesting evening at last, Richard?'

So she wined and dined him, noting with pleasure the open stares of jealous women and the sly looks of envious men. Twenty-seven years and she'd not lost her touch. She sparkled as much as the champagne she pretended to drink, gauging the moment when Richard could be persuaded to leave for the hotel.

It was a discreet establishment, used on the few occasions over the years that she'd braved the outside world and left Paul behind in the apartment. Tonight, the reception staff merely nodded politely, completely ignoring the fact that Amelie was all but carrying Richard across the lobby to the lift.

They got out on the second floor.

'Here we are…' Amelie propped Richard against the wall while she opened the door with a good old-fashioned key.

He stumbled over the threshold, then spun round, reaching for her. He pulled her close. 'Gonna give you what I wanted to,' he slurred, 'before you ran out on me.'

His kiss bruised Amelie's mouth. 'Bed,' she whispered, knocking the door shut behind them. Richard held her tight as she pushed him further into the room.

She broke free of him, kicking off her shoes and throwing her bag onto a chair. Next to go was the dress, slipping over her shoulders and sliding to the floor. Richard groaned and reached for her again, but she dodged out of reach.

'Not yet, eager beaver.' Amelie reached for the discarded bag.

The pink feather might have been made of lead for the effect it had on Richard; at its first touch, he fell back onto the bed and opened his arms to her.

'D'you remember the boa, Richard?' Amelie whispered as she straddled him, the tip of the feather running along the blurred contours of his face.

'You should have worn it tonight.' Richard tightened his hold on her waist and ground his solid dick into her crotch. His eyes closed and he let out a long, low moan.

That's when Amelie reached for the pillow.

#

When it was over, when she was absolutely sure the threat had passed, Amelie rolled off the bed, staggered into the bathroom and was violently sick.

At last, she wiped her mouth, lifted her head and breathed deeply as the enormity of what she'd done sank in. Paul had thought her strong, but he'd been wrong. Richard had almost bested her.

She stared at herself in the mirror, its unforgiving strip light revealing smears in the carefully applied make-up, scratches on her arms, a torn bra strap, and a faint shadow along her jawline. She'd come so close to losing…

Then again, maybe she'd already lost. After tonight, she'd have to disappear for good. For Paul's sake.

Amelie stared into the mirror. 'You're safe,' she murmured, pulling off the wig.

A tear-streaked, scratched and bruised Paul stared back.

'Thank you,' he said, his relief obvious as Amelie ripped a couple of pieces of toilet paper off the roll and began to wipe away every trace of her existence.

A Peculiar Circle
MATTHEW RHODES

Every Friday night I would take Beryl to the pictures and afterwards we would play Scrabble at her house. It was a tradition of ours that had lasted around fourteen months. Most people in Eyam assumed we were courting. I had to explain on numerous occasions that this was not the case.

'We're just friends,' I would say politely. Sometimes people would reply that we would make a good couple, or simply ask, 'Why are you only friends?'

I never liked it when I was asked that question because I was never able to reply instantly.

'I think Beryl would prefer it if we were just friends.'

Most people in Eyam our age were at least married by now. Beryl and myself were, I suppose, rather unique in opposing the norm. People were genuinely shocked at how at ease we apparently were with the single life. Like a twee rebellion.

I was anything but at ease though. If I could tell Beryl how I felt about her, I would have done. But I couldn't. If I told her how I felt and the reply was not mutual, I feared I would go crazy and lose all sense of purpose. Being completely honest, I had no idea how Beryl felt.

This resulted in the fourteen month peculiar circle we both drove around in. Like a laughable search to find something that was invisible.

I was left with two options. Either to carry on seeing Beryl for the pictures and Scrabble every Friday night or to just ask her outright: What exactly are we doing?

Being English, I chose the first option without much consideration.

I worked at a pub in Eyam. In between every drink I poured and every table I wiped, I would try and work out what I was actually meant to be doing with my life. Things would be far easier if someone just told me what I should be doing. My life was simply work. Beryl was the window to another world altogether. Beryl worked at the library. She seemed reluctant to leave the library, never mind Eyam. It was bizarre considering how clever she was. She could take on the world, yet she hadn't even conquered Derbyshire.

I often wondered to myself whether she had the same thoughts as I had. Why am I still here? Shouldn't I be doing something else by now? It was like our Friday nights were an escape from real life as it recharged its batteries.

One Friday night, I took her to the pictures and then we went back to her house and played not one but two games of Scrabble. As you can tell, we were living life very much on the edge that evening.

When I returned to my house that night, I poured myself a shot of whiskey and put the shipping forecast on. I always did this after I had seen Beryl. The shipping forecast was reassuring to me in a way in which I found difficult to explain. There was just something comforting about it. Almost therapeutic. The forecast and the whiskey allowed me to have a pit stop in the peculiar circle before I started driving all the way around it again to the following Friday.

So there I would stand on the balcony of my flat looking out at my home village before me, a shot of whiskey in hand. The street lights were the only sign of life and the shipping forecast acted as the soundtrack to it.

When the forecast ended, I would finish my shot and I would go to bed. I would always be able to fall asleep instantly. When I would wake up the following morning, the fruitless trek around the circle would resume and carry on its eternal loop of nothingness.

#

About a month later, a third option came to me from out of nowhere.

I decided I would tell Beryl what I was going to do the next Friday after we had just played Scrabble. I knew this was something I had to do. To avoid the damage if her answer to the *real* question was a 'no'.

It never really occurred to me that her answer to the *real* question might just be a 'yes'. It was more like a particularly good dream to me. Love was something that was simply reserved for other people. I was made for good spelling, being early for things, an excellent knowledge of capital cities of the world and for being nice and polite. Real happiness was something I saw in other people my age in this village. I accepted a while ago that I was going to have to find happiness and security within myself, whenever it wasn't Friday evening with Beryl. And whenever I looked at myself in the mirror and saw the gaunt, skeletal figure that would make my own mother wince, I perfectly understood why things had to be this way. It wasn't other people's fault. It's just the way the cookie crumbles, as my father would say.

The following Friday evening arrived and it was time to tell Beryl of the third option that had popped into my head.

'Beryl, I need to tell you something. It's quite important.' Beryl didn't say anything at first. She looked down at her hands before joining them together. She then looked back up at me. Beryl had eyes that could alter anyone's heart rate. For one very brief moment, I wondered whether this was really the right course of action.

'I'm leaving Eyam. I'm moving to Doncaster next week,' I said.

Beryl didn't say anything straight away. She continued to stare at me with those impossibly large eyes of hers and her mouth opened ever so slightly.

'Oh… I see,' was all she could reply with. Her response confused me somewhat at first. It was almost like the news had barely registered with her.

'I just feel like it's time to move on from Eyam. Doncaster has potential. It's even got a zoo now. There's no limits as to where it might go. Hopefully, I will meet my future wife there.'

Again, barely any response. I had definitely done the right thing, but I struggled to know what else to say.

'You'll be looking to settle down shortly too, I should imagine. I can't believe nobody has proposed to you already,' was the best I had to offer.

'As long as you are happy, that's the main thing. I just need to pop to the bathroom for a moment,' Beryl said very quickly.

When we hugged goodbye at the end of the night, Beryl still wasn't quite her normal self. She did say, however, that she promised to send me a letter every month and that I must write back. I said that I would return to Eyam to visit her in a year's time and that if I hadn't settled down with anyone, I would return to Eyam permanently after the twelve months were up.

I felt relieved more than anything on my walk back home that night. It was sad. Of course it was sad. But I knew it could have been a lot worse had I said something else to her. Beryl seemed more bothered about having another game of Scrabble and kept needing to pop to the bathroom. She barely asked me anything more about my plan to leave.

As was tradition after seeing Beryl, I switched the shipping forecast on and poured myself a shot of whiskey. I stood on my balcony and thought about my impending time in Doncaster. When the forecast ended, I switched the radio off and downed my drink. As always, I fell asleep almost instantly.

#

The twelve months in Doncaster were not a success. I made plenty of friends there. Then again, making friends had never been a problem. I found a job pretty easily at a pub. Doing the same as I'd done at Eyam. I remained single. I went on dates sporadically but nothing materialised. I began to worry about myself. Twenty-nine years old and still a bachelor. This was a rarity in this day and age. I was the elephant in everybody's room. The embarrassment of it all.

Being completely honest, I missed Beryl. More than I ever could have imagined. The best thing about my time in Doncaster was receiving her letters. It came as a relief to me when my twelve-month timescale had elapsed. I bade farewell to my friends in Doncaster. I knew already at that time that I wouldn't spend another day in the place. I knew what had to be done.

I packed my bags and returned to Eyam.

I arrived at Beryl's house without letting her know in advance. I wanted it to be a surprise. It was very late on a Friday night. There was nobody else to be seen outside. The village was practically asleep but Beryl's living room light was switched on.

Beryl opened the door and beamed at my stupid, silly face.

Shortly after midnight, we sat on the bench in her back garden and looked out at the pond before us. We each had a shot of whiskey in our hand and listened to the sound of Eyam at the dead of night.

'I should probably let you know something. Something that I've only recently realised. I don't think going to Doncaster was the right decision. Something I thought I would never hear anybody say, never mind myself,' I said.

Beryl finished her drink before me and smiled.

'What do you need to tell me?' Beryl asked. I finished my shot and cleared my throat.

'I've decided to live in Lincoln and settle down there.' Beryl didn't say anything. She merely frowned at me. 'I just think that will be the best place for me to settle down. Doncaster didn't quite work out but I'm sure Lincoln is the right place. An Italian restaurant has recently opened there! It must attract a lot of interesting people.'

Beryl looked towards the pond again. Everything was silent. It was like everyone in Eyam wanted to listen in on our conversation. The village held its breath.

'As long as you're happy, then you're doing the right thing,' said Beryl softly. She spoke so quietly that I couldn't really hear her that well, even though she was sitting right next to me.

'If for some reason it doesn't work out again, I'll come back to Eyam in a year's time. And I'll stay for good, I promise.'

'Okay,' she replied. Or at least, I think that's what she replied with. It was like someone had pointed a remote at Beryl and turned her volume down.

#

I didn't stick to my promise. Over the next sixteen years, I lived in various towns and cities scattered across the country. I lived in each place for twelve-month stints and worked at pubs over this period of time, and I would visit Beryl in between each stint.

I was well and truly lost in the circle.

I was still single. So was Beryl, inexplicably. By the time I was living in Brighton, we had both reached the age of forty-six.

It was while I was living in Brighton that something changed though. No matter where I was in the UK, Beryl would always send me a letter every month. However, I'd been living in Brighton for three months and no letter from Beryl had arrived. I grew anxious and started to think about this every single day.

Then, finally, a letter arrived from Beryl out of the blue. I tore open the envelope. She told me she was getting married in a month's time and wanted me to be there for the ceremony. She had found somebody. A man called Peter.

I went for a very long walk.

#

I arrived back in Eyam on the day of Beryl's wedding. About half an hour before the ceremony began, I sat on a bench in the church gardens overlooking a small pond. I sat in silence.

'This will be the last time you see me before I become Mrs Hurst,' said Beryl, standing in her wedding dress behind me. How long she had been there, I had no idea. 'It's hard to know what to say sometimes... it must be like going round in circles.'

Beryl sat down beside me and we looked ahead at the pond.

'I don't know if this is the right or wrong thing to say...' I said.

'Well, I'm listening,' she replied, smiling. I cleared my throat. For some reason, I couldn't look at Beryl when I said it.

'There's a new game called Travel Scrabble that has just come out. So now you can play Scrabble on the go. Like in the car, or on a train... good idea, isn't it?'

There was a pause. When I looked back up, Beryl was staring at me. I couldn't tell if she was angry, sad or, well, anything. It was a face fit for a poker tournament. She looked at me for the longest time. Didn't even blink. Like someone with that remote had now pressed the pause button on her.

She just carried on staring at me.

Then, she leant in, kissed me on the cheek and walked away from the garden without saying a word.

#

I left the wedding reception early. It was very late when I arrived back at my flat in Brighton. I immediately turned the radio on. I poured myself a shot of whiskey and made my way to the balcony. The shipping forecast played.

Beryl's husband looked like me. He smiled like me. Had the same personality. Had the same mannerisms. Had the same skeletal body.

The shipping forecast came to an end. I finished my whiskey. I went to bed.

I couldn't sleep.

About the Authors

Amy Bell was born in Leicester in 1981 and has been there in body, in spirit or both ever since. She has been writing ever since she was an unruly teen and has picked up an MA in Writing from the University of Warwick, a few competition honours, publications and performance slots along the way. When not scrupulously poring over her own words, she does the same with others' as a sub-editor; when she needs a break from all that poring, she knits, plays the ukulele and waits impatiently for inspiration to hit.

Chad Bentley is a writer from Blackpool but now living in Sheffield where he has recently completed a Masters in Creative Writing and is about to start a creative writing PhD. He has had both poetry and prose published in the Route 57 creative writing journal, including the most recent issue 13. He is also a playwright having had plays performed in various venues across Sheffield.

Lynne E Blackwood is in receipt of a second Arts Council grant to complete a short story collection based on her Anglo-Indian family history. She appears in the Closure Anthology alongside well-established authors. Her character-driven crime novel set in contemporary Republic of Georgia is in submission and she is on the INSCRIBE programme, developing her poetry for a chapbook. Apart from writing and editing, Lynne is learning to play the piano and panders to the needs of two cats and one granddaughter. Lynne recently visited Andalusia and explored wheelchair Flamenco for further performances of her work at festivals and events.

Simon Bland began writing a few years ago, taking inspiration from human behaviour and environment in particular - the prison setting he has worked in especially informed his ideas. He is now involved in the arts but this is the first time he has submitted a short story to a writing competition. He is currently working on a novel.

Rebecca Burns is an award-winning short story writer and novelist. Her first and second story collections - *Catching the Barramundi* (2012) and *The Settling Earth* (2014) - were both longlisted for the Edge Hill Prize, and she has won the Fowey Festival of Words and Music Short Story Competition (2013) and the Black Pear Press Story Competition (2014). Her stories have been listed for the Sunderland Short Story Award, the Chipping Norton and Evesham Festival competitions, and the Green Lady Story Competition. Her debut novel, *The Bishop's Girl*, was published in 2016 and her third collection of stories is due to be published by Odyssey Books in August 2017. You can read more at www.rebecca-burns.co.uk

Maureen Cullen has been writing since 2011 after early retirement from her Social Work career. She has an MA in Creative Writing from Lancaster University. In 2016, she was published along with three other poets in Primers 1, a collaboration between Nine Arches Press and the Poetry School. She won The Labello Prize for short fiction in 2014 and has been shortlisted at other short story competitions.

Lindsey Fairweather I was born in a suburb of Detroit in 1983. My writing history is long and varied. Most recently, I won a place on the inaugural Writers Centre Norwich/IdeasTap: Inspires scheme and was mentored by writer and translator Daniel Hahn (recently shortlisted for the Man Booker International Prize) as I polished my first novel and began a second. I have experience as a journalist (writing news, features, and reviews) and have also published several short stories. As an undergraduate at Yale University (from which I graduated magna cum laude), I studied Ethics, Politics and Economics, focusing on disabilities; I also studied fiction writing with Kate Walbert and John Crowley. After Yale, I moved to the UK and earned an MA in Creative Writing from the University of East Anglia, where I won a Malcolm Bradbury Award Bursary for my short fiction. In addition to writing, I have taught English at international schools in London, Vienna, and Madrid. I am married to a British diplomat; we have two young sons.

Bev Haddon grew up in Coalville and now lives in Leicester with her husband and two daughters. She has an MSc in Pure Mathematics and worked for many years as a reporting analyst (no, she doesn't know either). Her previous writing credits are a couple of stories included in Leicester's Big Care Write Up charity anthology. She is, however, a regular contributor to the Women's Weekly slush pile. When she found out that she had been shortlisted for "Leicester Writes" you would have thought she had won the Booker.

Katherine Hetzel has been an egg-pickler, weigher-outer of pic'n'mix sweets, bacon-and-cheese-slicer, a pharmaceutical microbiologist (the serious job choice), a mum, a learning assistant, and a volunteer librarian at a primary school. She's a published author who writes fiction for children (*StarMark* and *Kingstone* with Dragonfeather Books, *Granny Rainbow* and *More Granny Rainbow* with Panda Eyes) and visits schools to share her love of creative writing. She also writes short stories. She blogs about life and writing at Squidge's Scribbles, http://squidgesscribbles.blogspot.co.uk, and is a member of the Word Cloud, writing as Squidge and usually appearing as a rainbow.

Debz Hobbs-Wyatt lives and works in Essex as a full-time writer and editor. She has an MA in Creative Writing from Bangor University and has had over twenty short stories published in various collections. She has also been shortlisted in a number of writing competitions, including being nominated for the prestigious US Pushcart Prize 2013, one of two UK writers on the short list of the Commonwealth Short Story Prize 2013 and winner of the inaugural Bath Short Story Award 2013. *While No One Was Watching* her debut novel was published by Parthian Books. She sees herself as a writer, above all else, and writes every morning. In the afternoons she dons her editor's hat and critiques and edits professionally. As well as private clients, she also critiques and mentors for Cornerstones Literary Consultancy. See http://www.debzhobbs-wyatt.co.uk

A former journalist, **Asha Krishna** got into short story writing thanks to "Becoming A Writer" Course. Her poems and flash fiction have been published in online magazines. She lives in a Leicestershire village and loves her Zumba class. When she is not writing, she plays chauffer to her two kids, ferrying them across town.

Siobhan Logan's collections of poetry & non-fiction, *Firebridge to Skyshore* and *Mad, Hopeless and Possible,* are both published by Original Plus Press. They have been performed at Ledbury Poetry Festival, the British Science Museum, National Space Centre and British Science Festival. A hypertext narrative *Philae's Book of Hours* was published by the European Space Agency in 2016. Her short fiction appears in anthologies such as *Lost & Found, A Tale of 3 Cities* and the forthcoming *Mrs. Rochester's Attic.* Her story *Bodywrapped* was once choreographed by Belgian dance company Retina. Logan lectures in Creative Writing at De Montfort University, Leicester and blogs at:
http://siobhanlogan.blogspot.co.uk/

C. G. Menon has won the Bare Fiction short story prize, The Asian Writer prize, The Short Story award and the Winchester Writers Festival short story prize. She's been shortlisted for a number of others, including the Fish short story award, the Short Fiction Journal prize, the Willesden Herald prize and two Words and Women awards. Her work has been broadcast on radio and published in a number of anthologies including Fugue Press's Siren II and Dahlia Publishing's *Love Across A Broken Map*. She's currently studying for an MA in creative writing at City University.

Andrew Moffat has spent ten years working in international media and PR. Originally from Inverness, he now lives in Edinburgh. He has spent time working in China, Hong Kong, India and Thailand. He was longlisted for the Bristol Short Story Prize 2015. He is currently working on his first novel. *'The Child Kingdom'* is his first published short story.

Karl Quigley is a young, emerging Irish writer of Sci-Fi and Fantasy. He is currently attending the Creative Writing MA in UCD, Ireland and had his first publication in March 2017 with his fantasy short, Shadow Town. With an aim to create unique and awe-inspiring worlds, he is passionate about his writing and hopes to entertain readers in the years to come.

Matthew Rhodes was born and grew up in the historic Derbyshire market town of Chesterfield. At the age of 18, he went on to study English Literature, Creative Writing and

Practice at Lancaster University. He moved to Sheffield in 2011 and has lived there ever since. In that time, he has obtained a Masters degree in Writing from Sheffield Hallam University. Matthew specialises in writing surreal short fiction with dark humour. His main literary influences include Magnus Mills, Haruki Murakami and Erlend Loe.

Jack Wedgbury is a writer from the Midlands. He has a degree in Creative Writing and English Literature and was awarded the Creative Writing Portfolio Prize for his final year project. His short stories have appeared in University of Leicester's Short Story anthology and Writing Magazine online. He currently works for an independent publisher.

Thomas Welsh has won the Elbow Room Short Fiction Competition, and his short stories have appeared in various publications. His novel *Anna Undreaming* - the first part of the 'Metiks Fade' fantasy series - will be published by Owl Hollow Press in January 2018.

Marianne Whiting was born and grew up in Sweden. She came to England in 1973 to do a one-year course at Birmingham University. She's still married to the man who made her miss the boat home. Marianne has worked as a teacher, study support organiser and Sure Start Children Centre Leader. She began writing in 2000 and some of her poetry is published in magazines and anthologies. She writes mainly novels and her *Shieldmaiden* Viking Trilogy is published by Accent Press. Thanks to Dahlia Publishing she has lately ventured into short stories and one of her stories was included in *Lost and Found*, 2016.

Jon Wilkins Taught PE for twenty years, worked at Waterstones for ten, yet still like books. Coached basketball for thirty years. Wish it had been writing for thirty years, as it is, started writing seriously in 2011. Always wanted to be a writer, but other stuff just got in the way. Mores the pity! Anyhow, I've had a few bits published and have just self-published by novel, *Utrecht Snow* written as part of my MA in Creative Writing at De Montfort University. Married with two grown up sons, my perfect day is spent writing and listening to music. What a great life.

Farrah Yusuf was born in Pakistan and brought up in London. She writes plays, short stories and is working on her first novel. She took part in Kali Theatre TalkBack (2014/2015) and the Royal Court Theatre (2015) playwriting groups. Her short stories have been published in Five Degrees: The Asian Writer Short Story Prize (2012), Against the Grain (2013), Beyond the Border (2014), Love Across a Broken Map (2016) and Dividing Lines: The Asian Writer Short Story Prize (2017) anthologies. She was a finalist in the Writeidea Short Story Prize (2014 and 2015). She is a member of The Whole Kahani collective.

Judging Panel

Rebecca Burns is writer of short stories and fiction. Her work has been published in over thirty online and print journals, including The *London Magazine, Words With Jam, Per Contra*, and *Controlled Burn*. She has won or been placed in many competitions: Fowey Festival of Words and Music Short Story Competition, 2013 (winner and runner-up in 2014), Black Pear Press Short Story Competition (2014, winner), University of Sunderland Short Story Award (2016, longlisted), Evesham Festival Story Competition (2016, shortlisted) and Chipping Norton Short Story Award (2016, shortlisted). Her debut collection of short stories, *Catching the Barrmundi*, was published by Odyssey Books in 2012 and was longlisted for the Edge Hill Award, the UK's only prize for short story collections. Her second collection, *The Settling Earth* (2014) was also longlisted for the Edge Hill. Rebecca sits on the Steering Committee of the Grace Dieu Writer's Group in Coalville. She has been profiled by the University's Grassroutes Project as one of the 50 best transcultural writers in the county. She lives in Leicestershire with her husband and young family. Her debut novel, *The Bishop's Girl*, was published by Odyssey Books in 2016.

Divya Ghelani is a writer from Loughborough, Leicestershire. She holds an MA in Creative Writing from the University of East Anglia and an MPhil in Literary Studies from the

University of Hong Kong. She pens stories every day and has published in Litro: India, The Times, The Bookseller, BareLit, among others. Divya's unpublished manuscript has been longlisted for the 2016 Deborah Rogers Writers' Award, the 2016 SI Leeds Literary Prize and also received an Honorary Commendation in the Harry Bowling Prize for New Writing. Divya is the recipient of a Writing East Midlands Apprenticeship, a Literary Consultancy Mentorship. She is currently an Apprentice with London's premier short story salon, The Word Factory and will be a 2017 Word Factory Writer in Residence at Waterstone's Piccadilly.

Grace Haddon is a Leicester writer of fantasy fiction. She is currently in her final year of a creative writing degree at the University of Nottingham, where she was the editor of the class anthology, Vices and Virtues. In 2015 she won Malorie Blackman's Project Remix competition, and has since been shortlisted for the HG Wells Short Story Competition. She is on the writing team of The Big Care Write-Up, a Leicester writing initiative which produces ebooks for charity. Her story Zenith was included in Dahlia Publishing's *Lost and Found* anthology.

Debbie James graduated with a Bachelors and Masters in music from the University of Leeds and the conservatoire in Weimar, Germany before teaching and freelancing on orchestral percussion and drum kit. In 2007 she moved to Leicestershire to work for Premier Drum Company before deciding on a career as a bookseller. She opened The Bookshop Kibworth in 2009 and the shop has since won Regional Independent Bookshop of the Year, Vintage Independent Bookshop of the Year, Caboodle Bookshop of the Month and three James Patterson Awards for its work promoting children's books. In August 2016 the shop doubled in size, moving into a second storey upstairs. Debbie has run the Kibworth Book Festival since 2013, been a judge on the East Midlands Book Award and is currently Leicestershire's ambassador for the Booksellers Association's Bookseller Network and sits on their Independent Booksellers Forum panel.

Nina Stibbe was born in Leicester. Her first book, *Love, Nina*, was shortlisted for the Waterstones Book of the Year Award and won Non-Fiction Book of the Year at the 2014 National Book Awards, and was made into a television series for BBC1 and broadcast last year. Her massively acclaimed novel *Man at the Helm*, was shortlisted for the Bollinger Everyman Wodehouse Prize for Comic Fiction. Her third book, *Paradise Lodge* came out in paperback in March 2017. She lives in Cornwall.